A Candlelight Ecstasy Romance ®

"SO TO GET THE SAME REWARDS AS A MAN, YOU HAVE TO SACRIFICE YOUR FEMININITY. IS THAT WHAT YOU'RE SAYING?"

A dull flush suffused Jenny's cheeks. "Do I look as though that's what I'm saying?"

Logan pretended to ponder this. His deliberation took the form of a slow scrutiny that started at the tip of her boot-shod feet, moved up her long, slender legs, lingered on the curve of her breasts, and settled at last on her face.

"No," he informed her pleasantly. "You look all woman to me, and then some." The challenging gleam in his quicksilver eyes flashed a warning. "Of course, I wouldn't mind a closer look."

"Don't count on it." Standing up, she moved to put some distance between herself and the man who set off such disturbing thoughts. She was fast, but not quite swift enough to elude Logan's quiet reply.

"Oh, but I am counting on it, Jenny. I am."

A CANDLELIGHT ECSTASY ROMANCE ®

REACH FOR THE STARS

Sara Jennings

A CANDLELIGHT ECSTASY ROMANCE ®

Published by
Dell Publishing Co., Inc.
1 Dag Hammarskjold Plaza
New York, New York 10017

ISBN: 0–440–17241–1

Printed in the United States of America
First printing—January 1984

To Our Readers:

Candlelight Ecstasy is delighted to announce the start of a brand-new series—Ecstasy Supremes! Now you can enjoy a romance series unlike all the others—longer and more exciting, filled with more passion, adventure, and intrigue—the stories you've been waiting for.

In months to come we look forward to presenting books by many of your favorite authors and the very finest work from new authors of romantic fiction as well. As always, we are striving to present the unique, absorbing love stories that you enjoy most—the very best love has to offer.

Breathtaking and unforgettable, Ecstasy Supremes will follow in the great romantic tradition you've come to expect *only* from Candlelight Ecstasy.

Your suggestions and comments are always welcome. Please let us hear from you.

Sincerely,

The Editors
Candlelight Romances
1 Dag Hammarskjold Plaza
New York, New York 10017

CHAPTER ONE

"Don't try to hug the rock. Just keep your weight balanced and push upward with your legs."

Easier said than done, Jenny thought grimly. Halfway up the sheer rock face, it had belatedly dawned on her that only a candidate for the funny farm would get herself into such a spot.

What had looked so simple from the ground now seemed like sheer lunacy. People got killed doing this! This abrupt insight into her own mortality froze her in place. Her body pressed frantically against the cold stone as her heart pounded mercilessly.

A hundred feet straight down lay the rock-strewn shore of a mountain lake, its crystal waters reflecting a cumulus cloud bank drifting over the majestic Cascade Mountains of Washington State.

Above stretched another hundred feet of hard climbing before a secure ledge could be reached. Icy sweat trickled down her back beneath the flannel shirt and sweater she had donned so confidently that morning. Her fingers, clinging to a tiny handhold, ached. Her feet, positioned against the rock, seemed about to slip.

She was suspended between earth and sky, and her cornflower-blue eyes darkened with panic. Prepared though she had believed herself to be, the climb now seemed beyond her.

A sharp tug tightened the rope around her waist.

"Come on, Jenny. There's a good handhold to your right. Use it."

Her head jerked back. Dark brown hair the color of rich espresso spilled from beneath her knit cap. She glared at the man above her, the forward anchor on the rope chain whose sheer size and skill were supposed to guarantee her safety.

Some guarantee! Logan Kent was the most threatening man she had ever met. And considering some of the places she had been, that was quite an admission. From his sunburnished hair lying like glistening curls of shaved oak against his well-shaped head down his chiseled, sunbronzed features to the broad set of his muscular shoulders, powerful chest, tapering waist, and lean hips clear to the length of his long, hard legs, he epitomized all the intriguing differences between a man and a woman.

At thirty-five, he exuded a tantalizing sense of barely leashed male power founded on solid experience. He never hesitated to make his views known, forcefully, if he thought that was called for. And he had a maddening tendency to more often than not be right.

Just the mere suggestion that he accept her into his climbing school had set off a battle between them. Jenny still wasn't sure why he finally relented, but she did know that single victory was the last she won against the man staring down at her from the rock ledge.

His deep, hard voice lashed out again. "Jenny, come on!"

Some distant part of her mind understood that Logan recognized her panic and was dealing with it in the best way possible. While the small group of students and instructors was still on the ground, he had warned that the first-timers would experience exactly the terrifying symptoms racing through Jenny.

10

"You're all psyched up to make this first climb, so you think you're not going to feel any fear. Don't kid yourselves. When you get up there"—he pointed to the looming cliff—"there's going to come a moment when the potential danger of what you're doing hits you at gut level. We've all been through that and we don't expect you to be any different. So when it's your turn, just try to relax. Breath deeply and remind yourself that we would never have let you anywhere near the rock face if we didn't know you could handle it."

The other instructors agreed, their confidence spreading to the students who as yet had no real comprehension of what they were about to confront.

Now Jenny knew. Panic was a leaden weight inside her that threatened to tumble her slender body off the cliff and onto the sharp rocks below. It was the burning taste of bile in the back of her throat. Most of all, it was the intolerable fear that Logan would see her fail.

Unless she moved. Slowly, gingerly, cursing Logan Kent and his whole stupid mountain range, Jenny climbed. Miraculously, movements drilled into her during the week of meticulous training overcame even her dread.

Without having to think, she kept three points—both feet and a hand, or both hands and a foot—in contact with the rock at all times, balanced her weight naturally, and pushed with the stronger muscles of her legs rather than trying to pull upward with her arms.

And all the while, from his vantage above her, Logan offered quiet encouragement and instruction.

His presence was reassuring, she admitted grudgingly. He was so big and confident that it was impossible not to trust him. His large bronze hands holding the rope connecting them were poised to reel her in at the first sign of real danger and his heavily muscled body stood braced to take her much slighter weight should she slip.

11

But she didn't. Against her firmest expectations, in seeming contradiction of the very laws of nature, Jenny moved up the cliff. Following the route blazed by Logan, she inched higher and higher until at last the top part of her body rose onto the ledge.

A sinewy arm shot out, wrapping round her narrow waist and tugging her firmly onto the rock shelf. "Fantastic! I knew you could do it!"

Jenny's breath came in labored gasps, but she still managed to laugh shakily. "I wasn't so sure there for a minute."

Logan's broad grin flashed white against his tanned skin. "Could have fooled me. I thought you looked like a pro."

Jenny sniffed disparagingly. "Oh, sure. Then how come you started pulling on the rope and yelling at me?"

His smile deepened, though his smoky gray eyes turned suddenly serious. He sat down beside her on the ledge. "I was getting lonely up here all by myself."

Startled, Jenny glanced at him from beneath her thick, sun-tipped lashes. He was staring outward over the sweeping panorama of mountain lakes, ice-encrusted peaks, and far below, verdant wilderness. Though he wasn't looking at her, she had the unmistakable impression his senses were keenly tuned to her response.

The knowledge that Logan thought her attractive had been growing in her since they first met a week before. It filled her with contradictory feelings. When she first came to the school, and ran smack up against his hard-headed irascibility, she thought he would be the last man she would want to interest.

That was just as well, since she made it a policy never to mix business with pleasure. Her first venture into climbing was strictly in the line of professional duty. The article she would write about it was part of a series she was doing

12

on new challenges and opportunities for women. But over the last few days, the objectivity she had always before been able to maintain in even the most difficult circumstances had begun to be strained.

She had seen enough of Logan to know his forceful strength and masculinity were only part of his character. He could also be tender, considerate, and even downright funny in ways that appealed to her deeply.

But there was also a large part of him she sensed no one had ever been allowed to touch. The research she had done before arriving at the school strongly indicated that his only genuine commitment was to climbing. His relationships, well publicized by virtue of his penchant for models and actresses, were purely casual.

To Jenny, warm and loving by nature, he might as well be marked with a big red stop sign. She had far too much respect for her own vulnerability to even consider getting involved with him. Yet she could not quite still the yearnings he set off within her.

The result was that in all her dealings with Logan she was wary. The safest response to his last comment seemed to be none at all. Moving slightly away from him, she pointed to a massive snowclad peak in the distance. "Is that Mount Baker?"

Logan frowned, but nodded. "All 10,778 feet of it. About mid-size for the Cascades."

Having just managed to climb two hundred feet, Jenny could not imagine anyone undertaking a trek up something the size of Mount Baker. Yet she knew Logan had climbed the mountain, along with the other nine awe-inspiring peaks that together made up the spiny ridge of the Cascades. He was one of the last climbers to scale Mount St. Helens before the awakened giant sent megatons of hot ash down on the surrounding countryside.

That scene of almost incomprehensible devastation lay

13

far enough to the south not to impinge on the breathtaking vista stretched out before them. So enthralled was Jenny that she sat and stared for a long time before reaching for the camera in her pack.

The battered Nikon she used had seen service everywhere from the steamy Amazon River basin to the icy shores of Prudhoe Bay in Alaska. It had survived a crash landing in the Mohave, a flood in California, a deadly twister in Iowa, and an earthquake in, of all places, Connecticut. The camera was her talisman. If and when she ever had to part with it, she would feel as though she were losing a friend.

Logan glanced at it as she clicked off the first series of shots. He waited until she paused for a moment before asking, "Did you start out as a photographer, or were you a writer first?"

"Both," she said, raising the view finder again to her eye. "Nobody told me each was very hard to do well and that I should concentrate on one or the other. So I just went ahead and did what felt right."

She smiled slightly, remembering all the people who had told her she couldn't make a living as a free-lance photojournalist. Her family in particular had been certain she was foolish to leave a safe, if boring, job in the bottom ranks of a major news magazine to strike out on her own. They still weren't quite convinced that her camera and word processor paid for a condominium in one of Seattle's best neighborhoods, a fire-engine red Corvette, and a wardrobe that could only be described as extravagant.

"How about you?" she asked when she was sure she had gotten the shots she wanted. "Didn't anyone ever tell you it's crazy to climb mountains? There's this thing called gravity, you know."

"So I've heard. And yes, plenty of people thought I was

14

nuts. Still do, I suppose. It's just that scaling cliff faces appeals to me more than sitting at a desk."

"There are a few alternatives in between. Shark fishing, for instance, or polo playing. Did you consider those?"

He shook his head, his eyes teasing as they ran over her. "Nope, can't say I did. I just have this natural instinct to get as high above the rest of the world as I possibly can."

"Ever try hang gliding?"

"You mean in one of those little planes with no engine? No thanks!"

"You're not serious. You actually think that's more dangerous than what you do?"

"What I do," Logan insisted firmly, "is not dangerous if done properly. It only gets risky if I make mistakes."

"And you don't?"

"Not so far."

Jenny looked at him skeptically. She thought his attitude was a bit weak on common sense, but considering that she was depending on him to help her get down the mountain, she supposed she should be glad he was so confident. Now if only she could manage a bit of the same.

She was working hard at ignoring the sheer edge of the cliff dropping away only inches from where she sat, when the rest of the climbers joined them. They sat together for a short time, talking intermittently but mostly just listening to the haunting song of the wind soaring like a living thing around the rock face.

Logan did not let them rest for long. He wanted everyone back on the ground before the elation of a successful climb set in to distract them.

Jenny took a few more pictures as the rappelling ropes were secured around large, unmovable portions of the cliff. The activity kept her from dwelling on the descent that promised to be as challenging in its own way as the climb.

15

Briefly reviewing the fundamentals of rappelling, which they had all practiced diligently back at the school, Logan went down first to confirm the ropes were safe.

Watching his lithe, muscular body swing out over the cliffside, Jenny's stomach heaved. Dangling in space above a fall that could certainly kill him, he was relying strictly on the equipment and his own skill to bring him through unharmed.

Since there was no one at the bottom to hold the rappel rope outstretched away from the rock face, Logan's descent was the most dangerous. He had to maintain exactly the right degree of friction between his body and the rope while using his powerful legs to keep himself away from the jagged cliff.

No indication of strain showed on his chiseled features as he reached the bottom. Jenny suspected he wasn't even breathing hard. Through the telescopic camera lens she could see a slight smile curving his sensual mouth. He looked like a man thoroughly enjoying himself.

"Okay," Logan called, "start coming down, one at a time."

There was some momentary hesitation as the students decided among themselves who would go first. The instructors didn't press them. Having proven themselves on the climb, they could be trusted to make this judgment.

Jenny remained on the ledge taking pictures as her fellow novices descended. For each, Logan held the rope securely away from the cliffside, his long, hard legs planted firmly apart in the sandy soil of the lake shore. By the time the fifth man was down, a faint sheen of sweat showed on his broad forehead. But that could as easily have been from the warm sun as from any strain.

Only Jenny and two of the instructors were still on the ledge when her turn came to descend. Packing the camera away, she secured the rappelling harness around her slim hips. The ropes chafed slightly through her jeans. Ignoring the discomfort, she concentrated on easing herself off the rock shelf.

The wind picked up just as she pushed off. It buffeted her suddenly, causing her breath to catch. The rope curved under its force, but quickly steadied. Logan had moved back slightly at the first sign of increasing wind. The muscles of his powerful torso rippled under his natural wool sweater as he urged her on.

"It's all right, Jenny. Nothing to be worried about. Just hold on the way you were taught and let yourself slide down."

The panic she experienced on the climb did not repeat itself. This time Logan's nearness and her instinctive faith that he would not let any harm come to her overcame her fear.

Almost as gracefully as a seasoned climber, she eased down the rope until at last her feet touched ground. Her knees shook a bit as she let go, but her smile was exultant.

Logan laughed as he took in her expression. "You may claim to think all this is crazy, but don't try to tell me you didn't get a big kick out of that."

"Well, maybe a little one," she admitted reluctantly. More frankly, she added, "I usually do seem to end up enjoying the research for my articles, even if I do start out thinking I'm going to hate it."

"If you don't expect to have a good time," Logan asked as he rewound the rope, "why do you do it?"

Jenny hesitated, not sure how to answer him. She had never given much thought to her own motives. Whatever had driven her over the last seven years since she graduated from college and went out on her own after that brief stint on the magazine had seemed enough by itself without requiring examination. She was far more accustomed to devining what spurred others, rather than herself.

"I'm not sure. . . . I guess I just like the excitement and variety. I get to travel a lot and meet all kinds of people. No two assignments are ever the same."

"Neither," Logan said, "are two mountains."

Jenny shook her head ruefully, acknowledging that this time at least, she was bested. He had gotten his point across quite clearly. A challenging smile curved her generous mouth. "Well, even if it accomplishes nothing else, you can be sure I'll come away from here with a much better understanding of what attracts people to climbing. Once my article is published, you'll probably get hundreds of applications. You'll be more popular than you ever dreamed."

"God forbid," Logan groaned. "The last thing I need is more macho crazies deciding they want to prove themselves against a mountain. There are too many already. I spend half my time fending them off."

Jenny understood what he meant. Logan adhered to a strict set of standards for all admissions to the school. As one of the most famous and respected climbers anywhere, he could afford to be choosy. Only those he was convinced had both the physical and emotional characteristics to be safe climbers were let anywhere near his property.

Glancing around at the wilderness enclave, she could appreciate his protectiveness. For as far as she could see the steep ridges and secluded valleys were covered with a vast stand of trees, everything from pine and fir to maple, willow, and cottonwood. With the coming of spring, lilies, asters, lady's slipper, wood violets, and dozens of other wildflowers were in bloom. The air was fragrant with their scents mingling with the perfumes of wild ginger, barberry, and columbine. The wind carried the gurgling of brooks and springs released from the winter bondage of ice. They rippled over moss-draped rocks and collected into glistening pools where woodpeckers, quails, grouse, and raucous jays came to drink.

Beneath arching brows as dark as her glossy brown hair, her wide blue eyes softened. Pink-tinted, smooth cheeks framed a straight nose liberally sprinkled with freckles; vermilion-tinted lips owed nothing to the lip gloss she had long since bitten off; and her firm chin warned anyone observant enough to notice of her stubbornness.

Logan grinned ruefully. He was enjoying watching her, even as he wondered why he found such simple pleasure in the company of a woman whom he had originally intended to send packing.

From the moment Jenny walked into his office, waving the letter that had refused her admittance to the school and demanding that he reconsider, he had known he was looking at trouble. Everything about her, from the beautiful if unusual face to the gently rounded figure he wished were not so well hidden by her sensible clothes, brought all his senses acutely alive.

For once in his life, Logan Kent had been persuaded to do something against his better judgment. To his amazement, he was finding the experience rather pleasant.

But it didn't completely wipe away his doubts about her ability to endure the mental and physical rigors of the mountaineering course she was so determined to write about. All during the training period, he watched her intently, telling himself he only wanted to make sure she didn't get hurt. In fact, he just plain enjoyed looking at her.

From first thing in the morning when she emerged scrubbed and fresh from her cabin to late in the evening when she was often so worn out she could hardly stand, she enchanted him. Nothing in his experience had prepared him for a woman so genuine and wholehearted in her approach to life.

Slowly, hesitantly, he was becoming convinced that Jenny was just what she seemed—a lovely, intelligent, spirited woman who stirred him to intense desire mingled with tender protectiveness.

In doing so, she struck right at the bedrock of his life. Only the fact that she seemed unaware of her impact made it possible for him to cope with her at all.

To distract himself, he gestured toward a grove of whitebark pines. "Let's set up for lunch over there."

With all the students and instructors helping, the backpacks were quickly unloaded and checkered cloths spread over the ground. Maggie, the plump, middle-aged housekeeper whom Logan claimed actually ran both his life and the school, had assembled her usual "little snack."

Hearty roast beef and ham sandwiches on home-baked bread were accompanied by raw sliced vegetables and cherry tomatoes served with a crunchy sesame-seed dip. Lemonade and mineral water washed the food down. Peanut brittle and big, walnut-studded chocolate chip cookies were dessert.

After the hard climb, no one had any difficulty doing full justice to the meal. When barely a crumb was left, students and instructors alike lay back for a well-deserved rest.

Jenny's arms were folded beneath her head and her deep blue eyes were half closed as she gazed up at the cobalt sky. An eagle circled high on an updraft. Hawks also hunted nearby, but kept clear of the larger predators. Ducks glided over the pristine lake, bobbing at flashes of silver just beneath the surface. At the edge of the pine grove a raccoon scurried up a tree from where it could safely peer at the humans.

She sighed contentedly. Seattle and all the challenges of her hectic life seemed part of another world. Here there was only the soft lap of clear water, the whisper of wind, and the low rustle of leaves. That and the abrupt sense of Logan watching her.

Her eyes shot open. He was seated just a few feet away, propped up on his powerful arms with his long legs stretched out in front of him. A bronze hand sprinkled with sun-bleached hair lay next to her leg. A smile, gentler than any she could remember seeing before, curved his firm mouth.

"You look like this is doing you some good."

"More than some," Jenny admitted. "I can't remember the last time I felt this relaxed." She laughed softly. "Maybe because I've never been pushed this hard physically. There just isn't any energy left for tension or worry."

Logan stretched out full-length next to her, close enough so that the silvery strands of his hair mingled with her glossy curls against the deep emerald grass.

"You've just hit on one of the key attractions of climbing. Coming into close contact with natural forces and having to really push yourself to the limit to deal with them doesn't leave much room for anything else. When you stand on top of a mountain, you get an entirely fresh perspective on yourself, the world, everything."

A little sheepishly, he said, "I don't usually go in for a lot of philosophy, but I can't deny that one of the things that keep pulling me back to the mountains is the sense of myself as part of something beyond my own comprehension. That's a heady experience, however you look at it."

Jenny turned slightly so that she could see him more clearly. "I understand what you meant about macho types pitting themselves against the mountains, and why they're so dangerous. But when you climb, don't you think of yourself as conquering something awesome?"

"Oh, sure, there's a little of that. But any experienced

climber knows there's really no such thing as a victory over a mountain. At best, the mountain lets you briefly share a small part of its solitude and beauty and power."

"And at worst, it kills you." Jenny regretted the words the moment they were out. Considering that she was there in the guise of a journalist, they came close to being deliberately rude and provocative.

Fortunately, Logan didn't seem to take offense. He merely said, "Are you going to put that in your article too?"

"No," Jenny admitted. She had already decided the coverage would be upbeat in tone. After all, the whole purpose of the series was to encourage women to explore new ventures both at work and in their leisure time. "But I will include the usual cautions about being properly trained, never climbing alone, not taking on more than you're ready to handle. All the stuff you've been drilling into us."

"Good. It can't be repeated too often. Especially for women."

Jenny opened one eye. She regarded him warily. "Oh?"

"It's amazing how much meaning you can pack into one syllable."

"Don't try to change the subject. Why do women in particular need to be cautioned?"

"Because," Logan explained with exaggerated forbearance, "they're too likely to feel they have to prove themselves according to the standards of men. Whereas in fact they should be concerned only with establishing their own goals."

Chagrined at how neatly he had gotten out of that, Jenny muttered, "You aren't by any chance a closet reader of women's magazines, are you? That piece of wisdom could have come straight from several of them."

"Does that make it any less valid?"

22

"No, but the fact remains that women still have to function in a man's world. If we try to live according to our own standards, you accuse us of being impractical, emotional, flighty—all the excuses used to deny women advancement to better jobs or just plain respect."

"So to get the same rewards as a man, you have to sacrifice your femininity? Is that what you're saying?"

A dull flush suffused Jenny's cheeks. Even as she realized he was deliberately baiting her, she couldn't stop herself from responding. "Do I *look* as though that's what I'm saying?"

Logan pretended to ponder this. His deliberation took the form of a slow scrutiny that started at the tip of her boot-shod feet, moved up her long, slender legs to the gentle flare of her hips and the narrow indentation of her waist, lingered on the curve of her breasts just visible despite her heavy sweater, and settled at last on her face. By the time he finished, she was blushing unrestrainedly.

"No," he informed her pleasantly, "you look all woman to me, and then some." The challenging gleam in his quicksilver eyes warned her of what was coming. "Of course, I wouldn't mind a closer look. Maybe before you leave here, we can arrange that."

"Don't count on it." Standing up, she moved to put some distance between herself and the man who set off such disturbing thoughts in her.

She was fast, but not quite swift enough to elude Logan's quiet reply. "Oh, but I am, Jenny. I am."

CHAPTER TWO

The trek back to the cluster of rough-hewn lodges and cabins that housed the climbing school was completed far more quickly than the trip out.

Lighter backpacks and the downward sloping trail made the going far easier. The group of a dozen climbers and instructors skirted the mountain lake, following a trail that took them past the grazing grounds of deer, moose, and elk.

As they rounded the crest of the lake, Logan called a halt. Signaling for quiet, he pointed to the opposite shore, where a deer stood feeding. Beside her, two spotted fawns sniffed curiously at their brand new world.

The deer caught the scent of humans and raised her head, watching them carefully. Perhaps she was accustomed to climbing parties, or it may have been that the scent of a particular man who came there often reassured her. Logan was no stranger to the secluded glen, but he went only to look rather than hunt.

For a long moment the family stood poised for flight. Then the mother relaxed and returned to her feeding. The fawns followed her example and were quickly exploring the mysteries of fallen logs, moss-covered rocks, and rabbit burrows, to the delight of the wide-eyed visitors who watched them.

Later still, near where the trail led through a copse of

fir trees, Jenny spotted a moose. It stood majestically surveying its domain. The humans earned no more than a sideways glance from the huge, antlered male.

"It's a good thing it isn't mating season yet," said a teasing voice beside Jenny. "Otherwise that big guy would be crashing through the underbrush searching for a female."

Jenny had to laugh at Deke Broderick's eager grin. Though he was the youngest of the climbing instructors, he was also highly capable and experienced. His good humor enlivened even the most difficult lessons and made it easier to accept the inevitable toll of pulled muscles and twisted tendons.

At twenty-six, his unruly black hair falling in a cowlick over his forehead and his bright green eyes staring out at the world with unbridled enthusiasm gave him a rather endearing, little-boy quality.

Jenny suspected he made good use of it with the pretty young single women who flocked to the nearby ski resorts. But however much she liked Deke, she was immune to his charm. He was simply a pleasant acquaintance and a good instructor, though he'd made it clear he wouldn't mind being far more.

"I was hoping Logan would let me anchor you today," he said softly as they continued down the rail.

"Perhaps because I'm the only woman in this group, he had the most uncertainty about how well I would do," she said with a hint of asperity, remembering his comments about women's greater need for caution. "I suppose he wanted to be close at hand in case something did go wrong."

Deke brushed that aside. "You were ready to climb; there was no doubt of that. Some of the guys could have used Logan's supervision more than you."

But Logan, as she was quickly discovering, had a par-

25

ticular reason for looking after her. He apparently did not share her unwillingness to complicate what should be a purely professional relationship with distinctly unprofessional feelings. He wanted her to share his bed. With amusement that belied her serious regard for the problem he now posed, she wondered if he would compromise enough to share hers instead.

She was musing over that, with Deke walking quietly beside her, when the object of her unruly thoughts abruptly appeared before them. With a large pack strapped to his back, Logan looked even larger and more powerful than usual. Smoky gray eyes narrowed as he gestured at Deke.

"Take the lead for a while. I'll keep Jenny company."

The younger man hesitated, but only for an instant. He knew an order when he heard it. With a rueful sigh he did as he was told.

Jenny wasn't as accepting of such arrogance. Icily, she demanded, "What makes you think I want your company?"

"You prefer Deke's?"

Jenny bit her full lower lip. She was never good at lying. But neither was she about to give Logan the satisfaction of admitting she would rather be with him than the younger man. Instead, she hedged. "He's certainly easier to get along with."

The scowl vanished as quickly as it had appeared. A very male grin creased Logan's rugged features. "You don't impress me as a woman who likes things easy."

Jenny could find no response to that. She had to content herself with maintaining a determined silence all the rest of the way back to the school. Not that Logan appeared to notice. He walked along beside her, seemingly preoccupied with his own thoughts.

The lack of attention left Jenny perversely annoyed. She had never been one of those women obsessed with winning a man's interest. On the contrary. Except for social occasions when she was out with a man she genuinely liked, she preferred to maintain a cool, businesslike demeanor.

But Logan Kent shook that façade to pieces. Without even trying, he made her acutely aware of both herself as a woman and of the intriguing, if treacherous, attraction flowing between them.

When they at last topped the hill just beyond the school and made their way down to the cluster of wooden buildings, she was more than glad to part from him. With a cheerful smile for the other climbers, minus Logan, she went off to her cabin.

Logan's climbing school was nestled in a small, protected valley in the shadow of the legendary Devil's Summit. A large, timbered lodge provided ample space for the kitchens, dining hall, living area, and offices. Around it clustered small cabins for the students and instructors.

Some distance away, beside a fast-flowing mountain spring, stood Logan's own two-story house built of weathered cedar shingles and stone as rugged as the man himself.

Its sloping roof was visible from the windows of Jenny's cabin, but she ignored it studiously as she eased her backpack off and stretched before heading for the bathroom.

Like the rest of the cabin, it was outfitted with an eye to both comfort and style. Wood shingles sealed against moisture lined the walls. Built-in cabinets and shelves held fluffy towels, lotions for protection against wind and sun, and her own small supply of toiletries. The marble bathtub was big enough for long soaks while the shower offered pulsing jets of hot water ideal for strained muscles.

Jenny opted for a leisurely bath. She hoped it would help her relax and think about something other than Logan. But instead the seductive sensuousness of soft, scented water against her skin reminded her all too forcefully of the yearnings he set off within her.

After barely ten minutes, she climbed out and impatiently dried herself. Her wide blue eyes were unnaturally dark and her face was flushed as she pulled on a petal-soft azure sweater and tailored gray slacks. In no mood to fuss with her heavy mane of hair, she left it down in a shimmering coffee-dark cloud shot through with golden glints.

The dining room was already crowded when she arrived. Besides the two dozen or so guests and instructors, a party of backpackers was joining them for the evening. Jenny surveyed the group of six young men and women—all blond, tanned, and relentlessly wholesome—with mild interest that turned to sharp attention the moment she spotted Logan.

He had changed into a burgundy wool shirt that fit snugly across his broad shoulders and chest, and well-worn jeans riding low on his taut hips. His hair was slightly damp. It shone like ripe wheat, the lightness accentuating his tan. Logan was not a classically handsome man; his features were too ruggedly chiseled for that. But he possessed a compelling aura of strength and masculinity Jenny suspected she was not alone in finding far more attractive than standard good looks.

Certainly the three female backpackers made no effort to hide their interest as they studied him to the chagrin of their male companions, who seemed more than a little put out.

Forcing herself to look away from the sardonic stare that seemed to see right through to her soul, Jenny reflected that any man would have a hard time competing with Logan. Few would even try. None of the students or the visiting backpackers could match him. And among the instructors only Deke appeared willing to test himself against the older, stronger man.

Ruefully remembering the scene on the trail, Jenny resolved she wasn't going to be proving ground for either of them. Determined to distract herself, she headed for the kitchen to find Maggie and offer a hand.

The housekeeper greeted her cheerfully. Her plump, weathered face showed a slight film of sweat and the apron tied around her ample middle was a bit wrinkled, but otherwise Maggie Johanssen might have just started the day instead of having already worked some twelve hours preparing meals for several dozen people and overseeing the school's housekeeping.

"There's not much to do," Maggie assured her when Jenny asked if she could help. "The boys have set the table and carried most of the food in. I'm just finishing up the soup."

She had to smile at the description of tall, steely climbers as boys. Maggie lumped all the instructors and students together in one affectionately regarded bunch she treated like her own offspring. But Logan was held apart. Never once had Jenny heard the housekeeper suggest he was one of the "boys." Maggie had a deep affection for her employer, but she added to it profound respect. He was always Logan or even, in the presence of strangers, Mr. Kent.

Getting a soup tureen from the cupboard, Jenny teased Maggie. "I hope you cooked enough. Our visitors look like they've been subsisting on alfalfa sprouts and berries."

Maggie snorted as she ladled out the chowder. "A little plain, simple nourishment will do them a world of good. Seems like every year there's some new health fad, each stranger than the last." She waggled a finger sagely. "You mark my words, someday it's going to come out that all people have ever needed was fresh, honest food and plenty of it!"

Fresh and honest certainly described Maggie's cooking,

but plain and simple definitely did not. From the thick, creamy chowder full of plump clams and sweet corn, through the main course of stuffed salmon, hash browns, and salad, to the pear-and-plum pie for dessert, every dish showed a subtle blending of taste and texture.

The meal was as much a feast for the eye as for the stomach, but no one hesitated to demolish it avidly. After a hard day hiking and climbing, any food would have been received appreciatively. But Maggie's superb cuisine drew raves that made the housekeeper blush even as she tucked it in as eagerly as the rest.

Even the visitors admitted it was worth overlooking the obviously generous portions of cream, sugar, and butter that had gone into the menu.

"I can't believe I'm eating like this," the backpacker named Brooke said. "It'll ruin my figure." She glanced at Logan encouragingly, but he passed up the opportunity to comment and just smiled tolerantly.

"We'll have to hike even farther tomorrow," moaned the one named Lisa as she accepted a second helping of hash browns. At least Jenny thought her name was Lisa. She was fairly sure Brooke was the one with the long blond hair worn in braids, Lisa had the big hazel eyes focused appreciatively on Logan throughout the meal, and Jessica was the one with the smattering of freckles and the curvaceous mouth.

But the three girls looked enough alike, and the introductions had been so cursory that she couldn't be absolutely certain who was who. Nor was it any easier to tell their three male companions apart. Named Don, Dave, and Jason, they might have been brothers. Like the girls, they shared a youthful complacency that set Jenny's teeth on edge.

She couldn't help but notice that all the while they were talking about their travels through the United States and elsewhere, and indicating that nothing so mundane as earning a living could take precedence over their pursuit of "fulfillment," all their clothing and equipment was of the highest quality. Clearly someone was paying some pretty hefty bills.

Well aware that her disapproval stemmed at least in part from envy, Jenny told herself to stop being so narrow-minded. So what if she had always had to struggle for every dollar, making it through college on scholarships and seeing the world only by virtue of her work? Other people lived differently, and she shouldn't begrudge them their advantages.

Her resolve was seriously dented when one of the Brooke/Lisa/Jessicas managed to tear herself away from Logan long enough to purr, "How ever did you get interested in climbing, Miss Hammond? I'd be scared to try it myself, but I can see how someone with your physique would be terrific at it."

Jenny sighed. She'd never had much patience with catty innuendos. The idea that women were automatically competitors for any attractive man disgusted her. She refused to give Brooke/Lisa/Jessica's sally the slightest recognition. Instead, she murmured graciously, "Thanks, I am in pretty good condition."

Momentarily taken aback, the girl stared at her blankly. Into that instant of silence stepped one of the young men, displaying all the grace of a self-absorbed clod.

"Hammond . . . that name's familiar . . . weren't you . . . uh . . . in prison, or something . . ."

He trailed off, belatedly aware of committing a faux pas. Somehow it had reached even his notice that it was not done to ask brand new acquaintances if they were jail-birds.

That sensitivity, however, was not shared by all his

31

companions. "Oooohhh," squealed one of the girls, "you weren't really, were you? What did you do?"

Before Jenny could reply, as she was quite prepared to since she had faced the question several times before, Logan intervened. His voice was hard as he said, "Anything Miss Hammond did, or did not do, is hardly your business. You should have known better than to ask."

"Oh, I didn't mean anything," the girl protested, upset at having annoyed so desirable a man.

Logan cut her off relentlessly. Making no pretense that it was anything but an order, he said, "Let's help Maggie clear up."

Anxious to end the awkward situation, the instructors and climbers rose quickly, leaving the visitors no choice but to join them.

Jenny was annoyed that she hadn't had a chance to respond, but she felt curiously comforted by Logan's defense of her. He was so relentlessly independent that she would have expected him to stand by and let her fight her own battles. But instead he had instantly moved to protect her.

Being defended by anyone was a rather new experience for her. Reflecting on it, she settled in one of the comfortable overstuffed couches near the lounge's fireplace. The room, like all the rest of the climbing school, was rustic without being in the least crude.

Large enough to hold the thirty or so people comfortably, it still had a homey charm that in no way detracted from its essentially masculine character. Bookshelves lined several walls. Their selections included everything from the latest best sellers in both fiction and nonfiction to dog-eared mysteries, classic science fiction, and, of course, numerous guides to the intricacies of climbing.

The wide-plank floor was covered with a blend of antique Orientals and handwoven AmerIndian rugs, which somehow managed to look perfectly at home together. Scattered tables held reading lamps, but most of the light came from the immense fireplace that took up almost one entire end of the lounge. Surrounded by polished flagstone, it held a large oak log covered by smaller hickory branches, which Logan had lit before dinner.

The cheery warmth of the fire, combined with the comfort of the room itself, improved Jenny's mood. When Deke sat down beside her, she smiled.

So softly that only Jenny could hear, he murmured, "I knew you were too smart to let those little twits get to you. Just forget they're here."

Good advice, but not all that easy to follow. Glancing up, Jenny saw that the two of the Brooke/Lisa/Jessicas were ignoring their hapless companions and were perched on either side of Logan. Far from seeming to mind their attentions, he was smiling down at them. A frosty edge tinged that smile when his eyes met Jenny's. He glanced from her to Deke, whose arm had slipped around her shoulders, and frowned.

Undismayed by his obvious disapproval, Deke grinned. "Can't remember the last time I saw anyone get to the boss like this," he murmured into Jenny's ear. The intimacy of their position made him look like a man bent on romance, but in fact he was regretfully acknowledging the futility of any such attempt. "As long as I can't be on the receiving end myself, sweet Jenny, I wouldn't mind seeing you give old Logan a run for his money. He's had it all his own way too long."

Her back stiffened in surprise. She couldn't refute Deke's guess that he had no chance with her, but neither was she about to let him know she was interested in Logan.

"As far as I'm concerned, he can go right on amusing

himself any way he likes. It doesn't concern me in the least."

Deke eyed her with frank disbelief. "You should know better than to try to pull something like that on a climber. We're too sharp not to see what's been building up between you and Logan. Maybe you don't want to admit it right now, but it's there."

"So what if it is," Jenny countered. Anxious that no one overhear them, she moved closer to Deke. "Just wanting someone isn't enough for me. I need a lot more that Logan doesn't show the slightest sign of giving."

"Don't be so quick to judge him, honey," he cautioned, only to be abruptly cut off by the sudden blare of music. Logan had left his admiring fans long enough to turn on the stereo. He adjusted the volume to a soft whisper before walking over to the couch.

Blandly ignoring Deke, he held out a hand to Jenny. "Dance with me."

She shook her head impatiently. "I don't want to." Just for good measure she added, "Why don't you ask one of the teenyboppers?"

Logan threw back his head and laughed. His unbridled amusement caused starts of surprise from those nearby. Moving so quickly that she had no chance to stop him, he clasped her hand in his and drew her up to him.

His breath was warm against her cheek as he murmured, "Don't be bitchy, Jenny. It isn't becoming."

The sheer gall of the man stunned her. Flailing around for a cutting retort that would stop him dead in his tracks, she was hauled unceremoniously onto the dance floor.

Deke took their departure philosophically. Leaning back on the couch, he eyed the trio of blondes with faint interest, wondering if it was worth the trouble to get up and try talking to them.

Jenny tried to remain stiff and unresponsive to Logan's

touch, but he would have none of it. One big hand nestled in her hair as the other closed round her waist, the fingers just brushing the arch of her hip. Gently but determinedly he closed the small remaining distance between them until her cheek rested against his broad shoulder.

A shiver ran through her. She wasn't used to such large men, or to men so accustomed to getting their own way. Logan made her feel unexpectedly small and fragile.

That was ridiculous. Though slender, she was taller than most women and there was nothing delicate about her. Her assignments saw to that. She had no choice but to keep her body in good condition.

She had shot rapids, jumped out of airplanes, trekked through jungles, and run for her life in bullet-splattered streets. In situations where a lot of men would hesitate to go, she had proved herself strong, resilient, and more than capable. So why did she now feel as though a single puff of wind would be enough to blow her away?

Not even her stubborn pride could keep her from seeing the answer staring her in the face. As she watched the fascinating play of Logan's chest muscles through his shirt, a little sigh escaped her. The man was really getting to her. For the first time in her life, she wanted to surrender herself totally, to accept the powerful, driving strength of a man with all the softness in her.

She was too astute not to understand how this remarkable transformation had occurred. Never before had she met a man who inspired both confidence and passion. But trusting Logan as a climber was not the same as accepting him as a lover. While he would undoubtedly go to any lengths to prevent her from being hurt on a mountain, no such consideration would necessarily apply when he decided an intimate relationship had run its course.

Knowing that, however, did not prevent her from being acutely conscious of everything about him. Beneath the soft warmth of his shirt, she could feel the steely muscles of his shoulder. Her breasts were snuggled against the hard wall of his chest. One small hand lay in his as the other twined round his corded neck to touch the silken curls just brushing his nape.

His light, tangy aftershave mingled with the scent of clean wool and pure, unadulterated man. Jenny breathed it in appreciatively as she savored the easy grace of his movements. As the music grew even more languorous and romantic, his sinewy thighs grazed hers temptingly.

There were other couples dancing, but Jenny was oblivious to them. All her senses were tuned to Logan, heightened to such a fever pitch that when he spoke she jumped.

"I hope you're not upset about what happened at dinner?"

Mute, Jenny shook her head. She didn't want to think about their visitors or anything at all except Logan.

But he was not yet convinced she had brushed off the incident. Quietly, he explained, "Those kids wouldn't even be here except that one of their fathers is a good friend of mine. We do business together. He asked me to put them up for a night and let him know how they're doing. Since they hardly ever bother to call home, unless they need more money, he's been worried about them."

Jenny nodded, only half listening. She was too caught up in the sheer physical impact of being held so close to him to be more than distantly aware of what he was saying. Glancing up, she was surprised by the look of concern in his deep gray eyes. Her throat tightened as she realized he was genuinely worried about her.

Torn between amusement and appreciation, she felt called upon to end whatever grim imaginings were going on in his mind. "Logan, it's true I was in jail for a few days. But only as part of the research I was doing for an article about women in prison. It was a harrowing experi-

36

ence, but worthwhile, since I came out with a terrific article."

"Is there anything you won't do for a story?"

"Yes," Jenny said evenly, "I won't violate the law or my own standards, and I won't represent myself as something other than what I am."

"But you will take chances with your safety."

"I'll take a few well-thought-out risks, but I'm never reckless."

"But you do come to climbing schools."

She laughed softly. "Aren't you the one who told me climbing is not dangerous?"

He grinned, admitting defeat. "Okay, okay. You don't take risks. You're a model of prudence and discretion." Tilting her head back, he studied her for a long moment before he asked, "Do you know you're also extraordinarily beautiful and desirable?"

Before she could reply, warm lips touched the delicate line of her jaw, moving toward the lobe of her small ear. Jenny gasped as his teeth closed on it gently.

Fighting hard for calm, she said, "M-most of the men I know are reporters. They don't go in for a lot of compliments. Anyway, they usually see me in circumstances that are less than flattering."

"What do you mean?" Logan asked without breaking contact with now-throbbing lobe of her ear.

A flush heated Jenny's face, spreading down her slender throat and shoulders clear to the tips of her breasts. With a start she realized her nipples had hardened and wondered if Logan could feel them through the thin fabric of her sweater and bra.

"I—I seem to have spent th-the last few years on the job covered in mud or insect repellent or sand. . . . Not exactly conducive to glamor. And sometimes it feels as though I

37

live in pants. I've gone w-weeks without even seeing my legs. . . ."

"That's a shame," Logan murmured. "You've got great legs."

Since he had seen her in a skirt only once, the day she arrived at the school, she could only conclude that he was remarkably observant. Either that or just very adept at flattering susceptible females. For surely Logan knew she was far from immune to him. He couldn't help but feel the tremors coursing through her as his embrace tightened.

The pressure of his thighs against hers increased. Dimly, Jenny was aware of him guiding her toward the rear exit of the lounge, where a deck looked out over the rushing river.

She meant to protest, to insist she wanted to stay inside, but somehow the words never came. It was so much easier to just go along with him.

The cool night air brought welcome relief to her heated skin. A full moon floated low in the crystal-clear sky. This high in the mountains, the stars shone with startling clarity. They seemed little more than a touch away.

When Logan wrapped his strong arms around her waist, she leaned back against him unhesitantly. Such a beautiful night was meant to be shared.

For some endless moment out of time they stood together in silence. Neither felt compelled to speak. Their bodies, fitted so smoothly one to the other, were saying everything.

When Logan turned her in his arms, Jenny relaxed against him totally. His hand gently cupped her chin as he lifted her mouth to his. The kiss was light and undemanding. As though unsure of her response, he took her lips tentatively. No effort was made to force admittance for his tongue, but Jenny gave it willingly. She savored the taste of him and returned the caress fully.

Slowly, inexorably, the kiss deepened. It became a voyage of mutual exploration as they learned about each other on a new level. Jenny had never thought that the way a man first kissed a woman revealed much about his character. But now she discovered aspects to Logan she had only suspected. He was tender, considerate, passionate, and highly skilled. He showed no need to conquer, but clearly expected her to be a full partner in whatever they were to share.

For Jenny's part, she found a depth of response that left her stunned. Never had she so willingly opened herself to a man. Nothing was held back as she matched him touch for touch. When he eased his hold on her slightly, letting her take the initiative, her mouth claimed his as thoroughly as he had hers. Running her hands over the broad sweep of his back, she almost purred in delight. He was all hard muscle and controlled strength and thoroughly aroused male.

Deep within her a glowing kernel of desire exploded. Passion blossomed like a flaming flower, the petals tongues of fire threatening to engulf her. Part of her wanted to glory in the onslaught of her senses, to challenge them to the utmost and seek fulfillment beyond anything she had ever known.

But another part understood how easily such an inferno could destroy her. Already she could barely recognize herself in the trembling, ardent woman Logan held.

He sensed her doubt and shared it. What was happening between them was too far beyond either of their experience to be taken casually. They both needed time to come to terms with the astounding effect they had on each other.

Reluctantly, Logan broke the kiss. His eyes were rueful as he gazed down at her. "I think we'd better go back in."

Jenny nodded unsteadily. The silvery ribbons cast down by the moon heightened the harshness of his features, reminding her of some predatory idol impervious to the fragility of humankind. A flutter of fear darted through her, not of Logan, but of herself. She could so easily become lost in the maelstrom of need he triggered.

Turning back toward the lounge, she instinctively sought shelter in the light and noise and activity people always created to distract themselves from the ancient forces slumbering just beneath the surface.

CHAPTER THREE

In the silence of her room, Jenny stared up at the beamed ceiling. She had sought sleep for hours, without success. Alternating between shivering delight at the memory of Logan's caresses and worry over where it would all lead, she remained wide awake. The raw throb of desire he triggered within her would not cease.

Kicking back the covers, she got out of bed and padded into the bathroom for a drink of water. The face that stared back at her from the mirror was unnaturally pale, the deep blue eyes wide and mysterious. She ran her tongue over her lips, finding them swollen and pouting. Anyone looking at her would guess she had been thoroughly kissed. The more perceptive would see that she had also been left almost painfully unsatisfied.

Sighing, Jenny returned to her bed but didn't get back in. She knew sleep would be as elusive as before and she couldn't bear to lie there alone with her thoughts. On impulse, she slipped into jeans and a sweater, gathered up several towels, and headed for the sauna.

Entering the small wood-plank bathhouse, she hung out the sign indicating that it was in use, draped her clothes over a peg, and wrapped a towel around her slender body before brushing her hair out of the way.

The riot of glossy brown waves falling to her slim shoulders made her smile ruefully. Even cut in layers to frame her oval face, such hair really wasn't practical. With all the traveling she did, she should long ago have opted for a shorter, more casual style. But somehow she could never bring herself to part with the thick flow of espresso silk.

Lifting the heavy weight of hair high on her head, she secured it with a rubber band. The heat of the sauna would make it curl, but a quick shampoo and blowdry the following morning would take care of that.

Since the sauna got a great deal of use by bone-weary climbers, the hickory fires were always kept lit. Wet, penetrating heat struck Jenny as soon as she opened the door.

Removing her towel, she laid it over one of the cedar benches and stretched out. After the long trek of the morning and the even more difficult climb, her muscles ached. A thin film of sweat shone against her high, full breasts, small waist, and rounded hips as she closed her eyes.

Mindful of the need to remain only a short time in such intense heat, Jenny did not let herself drift off. But even so, it took her a few moments to recognize the significance of the sound that reached her through the mists of her thoughts.

Someone was coming into the sauna in complete disregard of the sign that said clearly it was already occupied.

She was reaching for her towel when the door to the steamroom opened and a stark naked Logan strode in.

It was difficult to gauge who was most astounded. Jenny froze in place, so struck by both his incredible intrusion and the almost breathtaking magnificence of his body that she forgot her intention to cover herself. Neither did Logan think to make better use of the towel he was carrying. They stared at each other in disbelief until both abruptly became aware of their compromising situation.

Fumbling with her towel, Jenny blurted out, "How dare you come in here! What are you, some kind of Peeping Tom!"

"Me! Why the hell didn't you put up the sign!"

"Don't try to pull that! I know perfectly well the sign was in place. You just decided to ignore it."

Belatedly wrapping his own length of terry cloth around his slender hips, Logan said, "I damn well did not!"

"Oh, yeah? Well, we'll just see about that!" Jumping up, she slipped past him and hurried outside.

Logan followed swiftly. He was right beside her when she jerked open the door where she had placed the sign. "There! You see . . . Oh . . ."

"Oh, indeed. Where is it?"

"I don't know. . . ." A sudden gust of wind buffeting the door informed them of the sign's likely fate, and Logan quickly closed the door against the cold night air. Acute embarrassment welled up in Jenny as she realized she had falsely accused him.

"Look, I'm sorry. I shouldn't have flown off the handle like that. At least not without checking first."

"Hmmm . . . you're right about that."

Something in his tone made her glance up. His hooded eyes shone like quicksilver. There was no trace of surprise or anger in his expression. Only clearcut, unmistakable desire.

Abruptly aware of her own vulnerability, Jenny took a step back. But she was too late. Logan was already reaching for her, his voice a low growl as he said, "I think you owe me something for that, and I'm in the mood to collect right now."

Jenny gasped as hard, male lips took hers. At first roughly, then with aching tenderness, he engulfed her in

43

the force of his driving need held barely in check since their earlier encounter on the terrace.

Her slender body twisted futilely against his far larger length. She was unusually strong for a woman, but her struggles had no effect. Logan's sheer size and strength overwhelmed her as surely as the fiery passion of his touch.

A low moan broke from her, giving the velvet roughness of his tongue full access to her inner sweetness.

As his hungry mouth devoured her, his sinewy hand moved down her body, relishing the narrow span of her waist and the gentle swell of her hips before slipping under the towel to cup her breast.

Gently, skillfully, Logan tormented her nipple to a hardened peak as he rained kisses along the delicate line of her cheek clear to the silken column of her throat.

"Jenny . . . my God . . . you're so beautiful," he muttered thickly.

The intoxicating delight of his touch broke her resistance. Even as she tried desperately to tell herself he had no right to do this, her body melted against his. A low growl of pleasure broke from him as her fingertips stroked the warm steel of his back and shoulders.

Stepping back slightly, he savored the beauty of the woman before him. The supple strength of her slender form delighted him. Her skin glowed like alabaster lightly touched by the sun. At the tips of her ripe breasts her swollen nipples beckoned his lips.

He obliged unhesitantly, giving himself up to the enjoyment of her loveliness.

Jenny's head fell back. Her eyes closed helplessly. A pulse began to pound against the whiteness of her throat. The vast, exhilarating world narrowed down to a single time and place. There was only Logan, holding her, touching her, making her feel things she had never believed possible.

Passion mingled with a growing sense of wonder as she stroked his massive shoulders and torso. Climbers were traditionally slender and wiry, but Logan was the exception. His huge body rippled with muscle. Not an ounce of fat lay on the hard planes of his chest, his tapered waist, or along the slim expanse of his hips to his sinewy thighs. Set on a journey of exploration made all the headier by her growing sense of feminine vulnerability, Jenny delighted in the raw male power he exuded.

Logan moaned against her heated flesh as his passion threatened to break all bonds. Easing a hand beneath her buttocks, he lifted her to him. Jenny gasped as she became unmistakably aware of his level of arousal and of what was going to happen unless she did something to stop it right away. . . .

Balanced on the razor-sharp edge between unendurable need and unavoidable doubt, she hesitated. Every cell in her body cried out at her to yield, to surrender to the glorious delight Logan could give her.

But her brain, ever the control center of her life, disagreed. It insisted firmly that she really didn't want what she thought she did. At best, she could expect to feel marvelous for a few minutes. But what about afterward? What about tomorrow and the next day and all the days after that? Stubbornly, it reminded her that she had never gone in for casual sex before, and that there was no good reason to start now.

Just this once, Jenny's body pleaded. *Let me not think just this once. The way he makes me feel . . . I can't stand it . . . Let me just enjoy . . .*

Once won't be enough, her mind objected. *If you have him now, you'll want him over and over again. But he won't*

45

feel the same way. It won't mean anything to him. He's had dozens of women.

Her desire ebbed immediately at the thought. How could she have forgotten? Only that morning on the rock ledge she had reminded herself that Logan's relationships were strictly casual. She was certain he never misled a woman into believing he was offering more than he did, but neither did he ask for anything but purely physical satisfaction.

Jenny needed far more. She had to be able to look herself in the mirror every morning without knowing she had compromised her most deeply held values.

A low sign of regret and frustration escaped her, "D-don't . . . I can't . . ."

The smoky gray eyes were glazed with passion when he finally raised his head. A nerve jerked in his square jaw. His mouth drew back in a lean, tense line.

For a moment she feared he wouldn't be able to stop and that she wouldn't be able to make him. Never before had she allowed a man to go so far only to draw back. Such behavior was deeply unfair to them both, but especially to Logan, who could not know of the powerful, contradictory forces sweeping through her.

"I'm sorry . . ."

The uncertainty in her wide blue eyes reached him at last. Slowly, reluctantly, he let her go. His frustration didn't even have the relief of anger, for he knew his predicament was more his fault than hers. He hadn't intended to so much as kiss her, and there they were almost making love.

That "almost" rankled. He couldn't remember when he had ever wanted a woman so much. Jenny did something to him he had never before experienced. She touched some essential core of himself that was even more fundamental than his habitual self-discipline. Another moment and he

46

had to wonder if all the refusals in the world would have stopped him.

But he was not a randy schoolboy out to satisfy only his own need. When he and Jenny came together, as he had to believe would happen soon, he wanted her to know every bit as much desire and pleasure as he did himself. He would be satisfied with nothing else.

Sighing, Logan moved back. Helpless to stop herself, Jenny's eyes ran over the vast expanse of his burnished chest lightly covered by golden hair. He was so magnificently male over every inch of his lean, rock-hard form. The woman in her—sensible though she was—could not help but be stirred.

"I really am sorry," she murmured tentatively, unsure of how he would react. It might not be too wise to apologize to a man left in such a precarious state.

Logan eyed her warily. "Don't bother. Any more of your 'apologies' and I'd have to spend the rest of the night in that shower."

Jenny blushed fiery red at his blunt reference to his continued arousal. It seemed to reinforce his casualness about physical intimacy and made her sourly glad she had refused him.

"I'm surprised you let that bother you," she snapped. "Surely it's an occupational hazard."

"What the hell does that mean?" Logan growled.

"Just that you have to expect some disappointments when you go around attacking women."

The gray eyes turned to molten silver as he stared at her indignantly. "Attacking! You know damn well that wasn't what happened between us."

Jenny looked away, ashamed of her unfair accusation and unwilling to look at the broad expanse of his chest. She didn't see him take a step forward.

"Or maybe you don't know," Logan murmured, his

voice dangerously soft. "Maybe you ought to find out what it actually means when a man attacks a woman."

Jenny's head jerked up, her eyes widening when she realized she was once again within easy reach of his powerful arms. She moved back quickly.

"Quit kidding, Logan. All right, I was out of line. But we both know you wouldn't . . ."

"Honey, I'm the furthest from kidding I've ever been in my life."

Jenny didn't wait around to hear the rest. Every survival instinct she possessed warned that Logan was in no mood for an argument. Perhaps later they could debate the protocol of lovemaking, but just then discretion was top priority. Grabbing her clothes, she fled.

She didn't get very far before realizing that dashing through the cold night air with only a towel on was not the smartest thing she had ever done. Beside the possibility that she would encounter someone, the sheer physical discomfort was acute.

However, she did not stop. Her abrupt departure from the sauna had surprised Logan enough to give her a head start. But he had recovered swiftly and was in quick pursuit. By the time she reached her door, only a few feet separated them. Not enough to let her get inside before he reached her.

Hard hands grasped her arms as he pushed her into the cabin and slammed the door closed. Shock and fear made her throat close painfully. She tried to protest, but was unable to make a sound as he yanked the clothes from her numb fingers. His bare chest was icy against her own chilled skin, his face implacable as he lifted her easily and strode toward the bedroom.

The realization of where they were going cut through even the panic that held her mute. Desperately, she twist-

48

ed in his arms, only to find that her strength was as nothing compared to his. "Logan! Stop it! Put me down!"

He ignored her. Without a word he dumped her on the bed and came down so swiftly beside her that she had no chance of escaping. Her hands were trapped above her head, her legs held immobile by a sinewy thigh thrown over them. Only when he was certain she was fully restrained did Logan speak, his voice a low growl that sent shivers radiating along her spine.

"You asked for this. I'm only giving you what you deserve."

"That's no excuse! I said I was sorry! You've no right . . ."

Her frantic protest was cut short as his hand moved along the ripe curve of her breast, over her slender waist, across the sensitive skin of her abdomen, to . . .

Tickle her?

He wouldn't. Oh, yes, he would! Helplessly, Jenny began to giggle. "Stop it! Oh, please, stop! Don't! Not there! Logan!"

"Admit I wasn't attacking you," he growled in her ear.

"I did . . . back in the sauna. Cut it out!"

"I want to hear you say it again."

"All right! You didn't attack me. Now, stop!"

"You wanted me, didn't you? Admit it!"

"No . . . Oh! Logan! *Yes,* I wanted you. Now will you stop!"

He did, finally. Jenny lay staring up at him, flushed and breathless. Although Logan had ceased his torment, her body was still trapped beneath him. She was acutely conscious of the barely leashed power in the hard male form pressed against her. Neither cold nor anger had been sufficient to dim his ardor. A dark flush stained her cheeks as she became vividly aware of how much he still desired her.

49

Instinctively, she tried to shift away from him, but the slightest motion brought them into even closer contact and further fueled her unruly emotions.

"Jenny . . ." Her name, uttered so huskily, revealed his own confusion. He was not, for all his seeming menace of a few minutes before, capable of hurting her in any way. But neither was he immune to the driving need she triggered in him.

Long moments passed as they gazed at each other. Jenny had not changed her mind. But the look in his silvery eyes—the tender, almost vulnerable passion—shook her deeply.

She had to say something to break the spell between them. But before she could open her mouth, the effects of her mad dash back to the cabin finally made themselves felt. She sneezed.

"I knew it," Logan groaned. "You've caught cold."

"No, it's just a little sniffle. . . ."

He wasn't listening. Climbing off the bed, he stood for just a moment staring down at the length of her body against the dark sheets, the glistening tangle of her hair spread out over the pillows where her arms still lay. His mouth tightened resolutely. With hands that shook, he pulled the covers over her.

"Now, stay there while I get you something to drink."

"I don't want anything . . ." Jenny began, only to be cut off by his impatient look. She lay quietly while he moved around the small kitchenette built into each cabin. By the time he returned carrying a steaming mug, her eyes were closed.

"Sit up now and drink this," he murmured softly, his arm sliding around her shoulders.

Too exhausted to be other than obedient, she did as he said. The tea was lightly flavored with honey and brandy.

It went down smoothly. A delicious sense of warmth and comfort spread through her.

She was only dimly aware of Logan lowering her back down on the bed and tucking the blankets in. A rueful smile touched his mouth as he dropped a light kiss on her forehead.

"Sleep well, Jenny." Determinedly, he added, "Soon it won't be alone."

CHAPTER FOUR

"So everything's going okay?" Kirsten Malm said into the phone over the din of typewriters clacking away in the New York offices of *WomanWorld*.

"Yes, it is," Jenny assured her editor, telling herself it was only a little white lie. In the week since the scene in her cabin, she had managed against her worst expectations to make real progress on the story. It was coming along fine. Only the nonbusiness side of her visit was causing her problems.

"What's that guy Logan Kent like? If his picture's anything to go by, we shouldn't look for you to come down to earth anytime soon."

"Oh, he's . . . about what you'd expect."

"That good, huh." Kirsten sighed exaggeratedly. "Sometimes I think I should chuck all this power and glamor and get out there in the real world."

Jenny laughed, knowing full well her friend and colleague would never give up the life she had worked so hard to achieve. "What about that art director, Charlie Davies?" she asked innocently. "The last I heard, you thought he was pretty terrific." And no wonder, since most of the women in New York would have given their eye teeth to stir the interest of the highly talented, genuinely nice, outrageously good-looking star of one of the city's top advertising agencies. Too bad for them he was head over heels about Kirsten.

"Hmmm." Changing the subject swiftly, Kirsten asked, "You're being careful on those mountains, aren't you?"

"I haven't been on any mountains. The closest I've gotten are a couple of cliffs."

"Will they look like mountains in the photos?"

"No, they'll look like just what they are."

"Oh."

Jenny bit back a laugh. Editors got very attached to their ideas of how a story should turn out. Soothingly, she said, "They're very steep and they have sharp rocks sticking out of them."

She heard Kirsten's little sigh of relief despite all the background noise and the static on the long-distance line. "That's all right then. Just as long as you're being careful."

"Afraid I'll slip and fall before I get past the rough draft?"

"That's unkind. Just because we're holding the cover for you . . ."

"Are you really? Great!"

"You deserve it. We've gotten a terrific response to that story you did about women starting their own businesses. If this series reads half as well, it will definitely boost our circulation."

"Does that mean," Jenny teased, "I should be charging you more?"

"You're already excessively well paid. However, should you ever decide to show up in the Big Apple, I can promise a very nice lunch."

"I may just take you up on that. After I get off the mountain, of course."

"Of course, but don't hurry on my account. Since I've gotten a look at the dashing Mr. Kent, I'll understand if you want to linger. Just make sure the manuscript and photos are in the mail before you get too distracted."

"Yes, ma'am. Anything else, ma'am?"

"Did you call collect?"

"Yes."

"Good. Since I'm paying I don't have to listen to any sass. So long."

Jenny was still smiling when she hung up. She and Kirsten had worked together for several years, usually thousands of miles apart but always smoothly and effectively. They liked and admired each other. The different scope of their talents kept them from ever being in competition, but even if that were to happen someday, Jenny was confident their friendship would survive. She turned away from the phone hoping Charlie Davies knew how lucky he was.

"I thought you were going to be on there all morning," Logan drawled. He was leaning against the opposite wall, watching her intently. "There is a lesson starting in a few minutes, you know."

Jenny could feel the heat rising in her face and tried hard to suppress it. Since the scene in her cabin the week before, she had done everything possible to avoid being alone with him. Driven by a combination of embarrassment and wariness, she was more determined than ever to keep their relationship on a strictly professional footing.

So far, she had been successful, in part because Logan hadn't pushed the issue. He spoke to her only in the line of duty and made no effort to seek her out away from the other students and instructors. In fact, he was so aloof that she had started to wonder if he had simply lost interest. Now it seemed that was not the case.

"Do you always eavesdrop on other people's conversations?" she demanded tartly, moving past him toward the door.

54

He made no effort to stop her, but kept pace at her side. "You were using a public phone in a hallway. How could you expect not to be overheard?"

"If you'd break down and put phones in the rooms . . ."

"What's the matter? Can't you do without the trappings of civilization for even a few weeks?"

"A telephone is not a trapping; it's a necessity."

"Says you."

The inanity of their argument struck them both at the same time. They laughed and eyed each other a bit more warmly.

"Well, maybe I was eavesdropping just a little," Logan admitted.

"What was so fascinating?"

"Just the part about me." He grinned mischievously. "Am I really what you expected?"

"No," Jenny informed him tartly. "I said you were what my editor would expect. She has very peculiar taste."

"Ouch." They were walking down the path toward the clearing where the rest of the students waited. Logan stopped for a moment, touching her arm lightly. "Look, you're going to have to come down off your high horse a bit. We're climbing together today."

Jenny's eyes widened slightly, turning an even lighter blue than usual. "I thought I was paired with Deke."

Logan frowned. "What gave you that idea?"

"The team notice on the bulletin board."

"Well, it was wrong. You're climbing with me."

Torn between the desire to be near him and the urge to be anywhere but, Jenny said, "I can't monopolize all your time. The other students will resent it."

She knew the moment she had uttered it that the excuse sounded weak. Logan knew it too.

"What's the matter?" he asked mockingly. "Afraid you won't be able to concentrate?"

"Not unless I can see where your hands are at all times," she snapped back.

Logan flushed. "You get nasty when you feel cornered."

"I am not!"

"Not what? Nasty or cornered?"

"Either. I just don't understand why you want to climb with me. Unless you think I'm not good enough to be trusted to one of the other instructors."

Logan's bronze features, which had tensed at her cutting reminder of his actions in the sauna, relaxed slightly. "I don't think that at all," he said softly. "You've made remarkable progress since you arrived. You have a natural talent for this and you've worked hard to encourage it. The reason I want you to climb with me is because I'll be taking the point. Seeing you up ahead will spur the others to do their best."

"You mean because they won't want to be outshined by a woman."

"Exactly."

"Well, if you put it that way . . ."

"I just did."

"All right, then. I'll go with you."

He inclined his head sardonically. "Thank you." Turning to the rest of the students, he said, "We'll be doing a little face-climbing this morning that will provide opportunities to practice the techniques you've been learning. Parts of the ascent will require bridging a chasm and traversing along a fairly narrow ledge. On the descent you'll be making use of the jamming and friction holds you been taught. Any questions?"

There were none. All the students were eager to get on to this latest challenge. All, that is, except Jenny. She stared up at the peak towering above them and swallowed hard. Not for the first time she regretted that she wasn't there out of any innate desire to climb. It would have made everything a lot easier.

"Any time you're ready," Logan murmured, gesturing toward the base of the peak.

The first part was easy enough. All they did was stand at the bottom and look. Logan insisted on this essential step of studying the rock face before making any attempt to climb. Jenny was gratified to discover that she could make out several of the better lines of ascent and some major hazards she was reasonably certain he would avoid.

Logan quizzed her carefully, pointing out as he did so several features she had missed. Only when he was sure she had a clear picture of the climb did he unwind the rope that would link them together.

Jenny watched as he moved agilely up the rock face. His ascent was so swift as to seem effortless. Not until she began to follow him did she fully appreciate how difficult the climb really was.

"Take it slowly," Logan instructed her. "Your whole foot shouldn't be in that hold. Just the tip. That's right. . . . Push down on that handle. Good."

Long moments later, when she finally reached the ledge where he was waiting Logan grinned. "That wasn't so hard, was it?"

"Oh, no. In fact I was so bored I could hardly keep my eyes open."

"Well, make sure you do on this next part. It starts to get tricky now."

Starts? Jenny swallowed hard. She thought the climb she had just accomplished had been difficult enough. The idea of confronting whatever Logan considered tricky did not fill her with enthusiasm.

But she followed along gamely, driven as much by her own pride as by the determination of the man whose lean, hard body moved so gracefully that it was impossible to believe he had any awareness of the sheer drop beneath them.

Jenny sensibly refrained from looking down. She concentrated strictly on Logan, ignoring even the sounds of the other instructors and students following them. As he began to move cautiously along a rock ledge that could not possibly be more than a half dozen inches wide, her heart tightened painfully. She was so relieved when he reached the other side safely that she hardly stopped to consider before following him.

But she hadn't gone very far when she began to see what Logan meant by tricky. The rock was steep enough to make any lifting of the feet dangerous. She had to shuffle inch by inch, her hands tightly gripping the cliff side and her body hugging the rock. By the time she reached Logan, she was breathing hard and drenched in sweat.

"Rest for a minute before we go on," he suggested generously.

A sharp retort rose in her, but she couldn't be bothered to utter it. It would only be a waste of precious breath.

"Now, this next part," Logan said a too short time later, "involves some bridging. You remember we talked about that?"

Yes, on the nice safe ground, and it didn't sound too great even there.

"I remember."

"Good. The gap we'll be spanning isn't very wide, just a few feet. Watch what I do and you shouldn't have any problem."

Unless you happened to consider it a problem to hang suspended in mid-air, one hand and arm pushing against the left side of a deep crack that ran up the side of the cliff, the other limbs counterpushing in the opposite direction. On paper at least, there was no reason it shouldn't work quite well. Jenny reminded herself of that as she watched Logan. What he was doing might look like the most dangerous part of the climb so far, but in fact the friction of his body against the narrow rock cut probably afforded him the best holds yet.

Jenny repeated that to herself as she started to follow him. The rock felt reassuringly solid against her and she found it was not all that difficult to gauge the amount of pressure she needed to apply. By wedging one part of her body between the sides of the cut and pulling the rest of herself up, she was able to make slow but steady progress.

Half the chasm was beneath her when she made a tiny error in judgment, her left foot slipped, and, knocked off-balance, she fell.

For a terrifying, stomach-twisting instant, she plummeted straight toward the sharp boulders more than a hundred feet below. The fall seemed endless, but in fact it was over almost before it began.

The rope tightened around her waist, breaking her fall so firmly that the breath was knocked out of her. Dizzy and gasping, Jenny hung suspended along the chasm, swaying slightly back and forth.

"Grasp hold of the side!" Logan yelled from somewhere impossibly high above her.

Instinctively, she obeyed. Her hands were cut and bleeding from scrapes and her knees throbbed, but she spared no thought for her discomfort. All energy concentrated on the single, imperative task of making contact between herself and something solid.

When she was once more pressed against the side of the rock, Logan began slowly and steadily to pull her up. Still dazed and winded, she was unable to give him any help. Only his immense strength made it possible for him to reel in her dead weight so quickly.

Almost before she could fully grasp what had happened

to her, she was standing on the ledge next to him, staring into implacable slate eyes.

"What went wrong?" he demanded.

"I—I don't know."

"You must know. You're just trying not to remember."

"I'm not trying to do anything except catch my breath! Leave me alone!"

"No! Think. You put a foot wrong, or a hand. Something happened. I want to know what it was."

"Why? So I won't blame you or the school?"

Beneath his tan, his face went gray. "Blame? Listen, honey, when you started this, you were warned anyone can fall. Anyone, anytime, if they aren't concentrating or they just make a small mistake. You may recall signing a release to the effect that you understood and accepted that. So don't talk to me about blame. If I hadn't been here, you'd be lying down there right now."

Remorselessly, he pointed to the sharp rocks far below. Jenny was helpless to keep her eyes from following the direction of his hand. Fresh waves of dizziness swept over her as she stared at what could have been her grave. Her face drained of color and her body trembled, as though buffeted by a high wind.

"What the hell are you doing?" an angry voice demanded from just below them. "Can't you see how upset she is?"

"Stay out of this, Deke," Logan ordered. "You've got your own student to attend to."

"*My* student is fine. It's yours who looks like she's about to topple over."

Swift movements brought the younger man to Jenny's side. He looked at her worriedly. "Are you all right? Did you get hurt?"

Numbly, she shook her head. Logan's seeming callousness had brought her close to tears, but she was damned if she would let him see them. Hoarsely, she murmured, "N-no . . . I was just scared."

"Of course you were," Deke said gently. "Anybody would be. Here, let me help you." He reached out a hand to steady her, only to be stopped by a peremptory order from Logan.

"You know you're not supposed to leave a student unsupervised. Get back down the side."

There was no mistaking the anger in his tone, but still Deke hesitated. It was left to Jenny to put a stop to the confrontation.

"It's all right," she murmured. "I'm fine, really."

"Are you sure?"

"Yes, go on now." Softly, she repeated, "I'm fine."

Deke was clearly still not convinced, but he could not fight both his boss's dictates and Jenny's assurances. Reluctantly, he lowered himself back down the side of the cliff.

When they were alone again, she faced Logan indignantly. Even the memory of her close brush with death was eclipsed by her anger. Furiously, she demanded, "Why did you have to talk to him like that? He was only trying to help."

"In a pig's eye," Logan snarled. "He was interfering, and if he does it again, I'll damn well can him."

"That's a great attitude! What's the matter, don't you think he's tough enough just because he isn't afraid to show a little compassion?"

"Is that what you think he was showing, compassion?" Logan laughed harshly. "You may be a terrific reporter, but you sure have a hell of a lot to learn about men. Or maybe you wouldn't mind being on the receiving end of a little of Deke's brand of . . . compassion."

"Y-you . . ." For once in her life, words failed Jenny. She could only grit her teeth powerlessly as she struggled

61

to find some way to express her utter contempt for anyone who could twist consideration and concern into something self-serving.

"I can't talk to you," she said at last. "You're an arrogant, insensitive boor and I don't want anything more to do with you. Just get me off this mountain."

Logan's big hands clenched at his sides. His firm mouth drew back in an angry snarl. "And how do you expect me to do that if you don't want to have anything more to do with me?" he taunted.

Jenny thought she had reached the nadir of panic at the moment when she lost her footing and fell into space, but she realized now that was not the case. As the meaning of his words sank in, she stared at him in horror. "You don't mean . . . You wouldn't . . ."

"Leave you here? No, I wouldn't. Although I have to admit it's a temptation. But you started this climb and you're damn well going to finish it if I have to push you down every inch of this cliff myself."

Jenny believed him perfectly capable of doing just that. His eyes were so cold and his manner so remorseless that she knew she had no choice but to do as he said. Grimly, refusing to let him see how hurt and frightened she was, she followed his instructions to the letter. The climb down seemed to take forever, but not for a moment did she consider asking him to go slower or let her rest. All she could think of was getting off the rock face and away from Logan as fast as she possibly could.

The moment they reached the bottom, she untied the rope from around her waist, dropped it to the ground, and walked as quickly as her shaking legs would carry her back toward the school. In the back of her mind was the memory of how Logan had reacted when she fled from him the week before. But this time he made no effort to come after her. She reached the privacy of her cabin without interference.

Once inside with the door safely closed behind her, she collapsed on the bed. The tears of fright and pain she had only just managed to hold back until she was alone burst free with a vengeance. She sobbed softly, rocking back and forth with her arms wrapped around herself and her head bent.

Long moments later, when the worst of her terror had spent itself, she slowly became aware of the touch of a cool hand on her brow. Startled, she looked up. Logan stood over her, his features calm and composed and his voice steady. "Are you willing to listen to me now?"

Shocked by his sudden appearance at such a vulnerable moment, not stopping to ask why he was there, Jenny lashed out at him in rage. "Go away! I don't want you here! You don't have any right to see me like this! Go away!"

Her tirade left him unmoved. He simply waited patiently until she wore herself out, then eased her into his arms. "Hush, Jenny," he murmured, "you're safe now. Everything's going to be all right. Hush."

The words were comforting in themselves, but it was his tone that reached her most clearly. She had never heard him sound so gentle and consoling.

Baffled, she put aside her fury long enough to ask, "W-why are you being so kind now when back there . . . on the cliff . . . you didn't care how I felt?"

"That isn't true," he murmured against the silken fall of her hair. "I did care very much. When I saw you fall, I . . . Well, let's just say I can't remember the last time I was that scared. Of course I wanted to comfort you. But halfway up the side of a cliff is not the place to be sympathetic." Tilting her head back, he stared into her indigo eyes as he asked, "If I had let you release all your fear right

63

there, instead of waiting, would you have been in any shape to climb down?"

"No," Jenny admitted shakily. She was beginning to see what had caused him to behave as he had. But she still wasn't quite ready to admit he had been right. "Why were you so mean to Deke when he was only trying to help?"

"Because it was bad enough that he left his own student without also encouraging you to give in to your feelings right there." Tightly, he added, "He's a good instructor and he certainly knows better than to behave like that. Or at least he will when I get through having a talk with him."

Anxiously, Jenny asked, "You don't really mean to fire him?"

"No," Logan admitted, "I don't. But neither will I stand for another display like that. He endangered both his own student and you. It can't happen again."

Though she privately wondered if Logan's annoyance with the younger man stemmed strictly from professional concerns, she refrained from voicing her doubts. Instead, she remained silent as he insisted on checking the abrasions on her hands and arms.

"You need a first-aid cream on these. Do you have any here?"

"No, but they aren't really that serious, are they? I'll just wash them off and . . ."

"You'll just come along to the office so I can take care of them properly."

Determinedly, he guided her out of the cabin and down the path to the main building. The rest of the students and instructors were in their own quarters, recovering from the day's exercise, so it was very quiet. The wind rustled gently through the trees and a thrush sang softly as Logan opened the office door and followed her inside.

Gesturing to the far corner of the room, he said, "The bath is over there. Come on."

Logan might claim to believe that a telephone was an unnecessary trapping of civilization, but Jenny couldn't help but notice that when it came to certain physical comforts he didn't stint. The bath he led her to was small and unmistakably masculine, but it was also the last word in luxury.

Completely lined in cedar with a red brick floor, it was outfitted with black marble fixtures and dominated by a huge mirrored cabinet that took up all of one wall. From it, Logan took a first-aid kit. He watched critically as Jenny washed her hands and arms, then carefully applied cream to the scrapes before covering the worst ones with light gauze bandages.

His touch was impersonal, but she still could not stop the clamoring of her senses responding to his nearness. By the time he finished, it was all she could do not to reach out and touch the large hands that moved over her so gently.

"That should do it," he said at last, his voice just a bit gruff. As he looked up, their eyes met. Jenny was startled by the tenderness she saw there. The knowledge that he really did care about what had happened to her brought a fresh wave of tears. She blinked against them fiercely, but to no avail. To her dismay, they began to trickle down her pale cheeks.

"I don't know what's wrong with me," she muttered thickly. "I never cry."

Logan touched a finger to her face, catching a tear. So softly that she could barely hear him, he murmured, "Why not?"

"B-because it's weak to cry."

"Is it?"

"Yes. I'll bet you never cry."

65

A tiny smile curved his mouth. "You lose."

"I . . . don't believe you."

"It's true. Oh, I admit, I can't manage to do it quite as . . . vigorously as you. But I've been known to shed a tear from time to time." Moving closer to her, his big hands cupping her face, he murmured, "Why shouldn't a man be able to cry? I'm human too, you know."

Oh, yes, she did know. Every part of her knew. He was warm and solid and very, very real. Tentatively, unsure of her own motives or his likely response, she reached out to touch him. Her hand brushed the hard line of his jaw, moving over bronze skin lightly roughened by the stubble of his beard.

Logan sighed softly. He shifted slightly, enough to bring them closer together. Slowly, giving her plenty of time to withdraw, he bent his lips to hers.

His kiss was infinitely gentle and undemanding. It spoke far more of comfort than desire, yet it was nonetheless overwhelmingly exciting. A man, Jenny was discovering, could be passionate in many ways. The tenderness he showed stirred her deeply. Of her own accord she lifted her hands to the thick softness of his hair, running lightly over the silken strands before trailing down the broad width of his shoulders to the powerful muscles of his back.

"Jenny . . ."

"Hmmm."

"Do you know what you do to me?"

She laughed softly, heady with the sense of her own power. "The same thing you do to me, I hope."

His mouth hardened slightly, parting her lips so that his tongue could probe the moist sweetness they guarded. The tremor that ran through them both warned that neither could take much more without going far further.

Withdrawing just enough to be able to look at her,

Logan said gently, "I've never made love in a bathroom. It doesn't strike me as very comfortable."

Confusion darted through Jenny's eyes. She wanted him so badly that she hurt inside, yet none of the reasons that had kept her from being intimate with him the week before had been resolved. Would Logan think she had simply led him on again?

He saw the concern that darkened her gaze and smiled tenderly. "Don't worry. I know you're not ready for that yet, in the bathroom or otherwise. Believe me, I have no intention of repeating my mistake of last week and trying to rush you. However . . ."

Standing up, he drew her with him, holding her close as he said, "Have dinner with me tonight, Jenny. Away from the school. I think it's time we started to get to know each other without so many other people around."

She hadn't forgotten her instinctive conviction that she should be wary of him, nor had she lost sight of her objection to mixing business and pleasure. All of that remained strong within her. But none of it seemed to matter very much as she softly accepted his invitation.

CHAPTER FIVE

When she packed for her trip, Jenny had hesitated about including anything other than sensible pants and warm tops. But at the last minute some impulse caused her to drop in a blue silk dress, which she promptly told herself she would have no opportunity to wear.

Now she did. Back in her cabin she showered and washed her hair, blowing it dry so that it fell in a gleaming curtain to her shoulders. The sun had added silvery glints to the rich dark strands. A soft apricot tinge warmed her skin. There was a smattering of freckles over her nose, but she saw no reason to try to cover them up. Instead, she was satisfied with no more than a good moisturizer, a touch of indigo-blue shadow above her eyes, and a soft vermilion lip cream. Spraying on a jasmine-scented perfume that was her favorite, she slipped into lacy underwear before dropping the dress over her head.

Shoes might have been a problem if she hadn't also packed a pair of slim black pumps that complemented the slender line of her legs beneath the knee-length hem. She hadn't brought any jewelry, but glancing at herself in the mirror, she realized she didn't need any. Excitement gave a radiant glow to her features. She was looking forward to her date with Logan, and she wasn't going to let any doubts about the wisdom of what she was doing spoil her enjoyment.

When he knocked, she was ready. Opening the cabin door, she stood for a moment drinking in the sight of him elegantly attired in dark gray slacks, a pearly white shirt, and a blue blazer that in no way hid the powerful sweep of his shoulders and chest. In the rugged clothes he wore for climbing he always looked extremely attractive. But she was not prepared for the impact of polished urbanity coupled with compelling virility. She caught herself wondering how many men could so effortlessly combine the two.

Her surprise at his transformation was matched by his own. Slate-gray eyes wandered over her appreciatively as he said, "You should have warned me. I was sure you'd look lovely, but I had no idea . . ."

His voice trailed off as he remained on the doorstep, ignoring her silent invitation to come in. Jenny got her coat and bag before joining him outside. They walked in silence to the jeep parked a short distance away.

He helped her in, then went around to the other side to get behind the wheel. Adroitly maneuvering down the gravel driveway, he soon had them on the main road.

"Do you always drive this?" Jenny asked when they had gone about a quarter of a mile from the school.

"Yes, it's really the only practical vehicle on some of the roads around here." Glancing at her, he added, "I hope you don't mind. It doesn't exactly go with your outfit."

"What? Oh, no, of course I don't mind." She laughed softly at the idea that she might somehow be offended by their utilitarian transport. "I've ridden in some things that make this look like a Rolls."

Logan grinned. The tension that had been in him from the moment she opened the cabin door eased slightly. "Tell me about them."

"You don't really want to hear the litany of places I've been?"

69

"Yes, I do."

Reluctantly, Jenny gave in. For the rest of the drive she regaled him with stories about elephant rides in India, white-water rafting in Colorado, hot-air ballooning over the French countryside, and even a trip she had taken the year before on the Orient Express to write about the revival of that legendary train.

Logan listened attentively. He seemed genuinely interested and asked intelligent questions about places and people that revealed the scope of his own curiosity. As they pulled up in front of the restaurant, he said, "I thought I'd been around a lot. But you've seen places I've only dreamed about. I have to admit, I envy you."

"But I always stay as close to sea level as I can get," Jenny teased. "If you traveled with me, you'd be awfully bored."

As she realized what she had just said, a blush spread over her cheeks. Logan grinned engagingly. "I doubt it," he said, "but maybe we should take a trip together and find out."

It was impossible to tell if he was at all serious, and there was no subtle enough way to ask. Fortunately, the maître d' arrived at that moment to escort them to the table Logan had reserved.

The inn was at once rustic and elegant. Tables spaced far enough apart to afford privacy were covered with glistening white linen and set with Delft china, crystal, and silver. Bouquets of wild flowers were framed by candles in pewter holders. The evening was cool enough to allow for a fire, which lent a warm, cheerful air to the surroundings.

Over a pre-dinner glass of white wine, Jenny said, "I did some research before getting in touch with you that indicated you'd been pretty much all over the world. You must have started traveling when you were very young."

"Right out of high school." Logan grinned, the candlelight adding a burnished glow to his high-boned features. "As soon as I turned eighteen, I decided Boston had nothing more to offer me. I considered joining the army to see the world. But that seemed too easy, so I signed up with the marines instead."

"Were you in . . ."

"Vietnam? Yes, I got sent there straight out of bootcamp." He grimaced faintly. "A friend of mine who's a shrink claims it isn't a coincidence that I started climbing as soon as I got back." Taking a sip of his Scotch and water, he added, "I'm not sure he isn't right. But I know I got off fairly easy. I came back in one piece, which is more than a lot of the guys can say."

"What did your family think of your going?" Jenny asked softly, trying not to give in to the painful images his revelation raised in her.

"They were horrified," he admitted. "I was supposed to go straight on to college, then grad school, get a nice law degree, and settle down just like every other male in my family for about the last hundred years." He shrugged lightly. "But that just wasn't for me. And fortunately, they were able to accept it."

"You ended up at the University of Colorado," Jenny recalled.

"Only because it had a climbing course. I spent a lot more time on mountains than I did in classrooms. But I still got a good enough education to figure out I had an awful lot to learn. That's when I started traveling."

Looking at her closely, he said, "You've got the advantage over me. I don't have the benefit of background research. But let me take a few guesses anyway."

He leaned back in his chair, the glass of amber liquid held easily between his lean fingers. Jenny waited with greater interest than she carried to admit to hear what he would say.

"You grew up in the East . . . I can hear just the slightest hint of it in your speech. Not New York though. Philadelphia?"

Flabbergasted, she nodded. "How did you know that? There's no such thing as a Philadelphia accent."

"All regions have their own speech patterns," he insisted. "With the influence of television I suppose we'll all end up sounding the same. But right now you can still catch telltale signs, if you know what to listen for."

The waiter interrupted for a moment to ask if they wanted another round. Jenny shook her head, prompting Logan to request the menus. When they were alone again, he went on. "So, you were born and raised in Philadelphia, but you haven't lived there in a while. My guess is you got out as soon as you could, the same way I did. College . . . on the West Coast. Seattle?"

"Right, but I can see how you figured that out, since I live there now."

"Not all the time though. You travel a lot. What I want to know is how you worked your way into a job that gives you so much freedom."

Jenny laughed, thinking back to those hectic days when she was first striking out on her own. "I didn't exactly work my way into it. It was more a case of jumping headfirst."

Logan raised an eyebrow quizzically, encouraging her to explain. "When I got out of college, I was lucky enough to get a job as a researcher on a major news magazine in New York. It was a break a lot of people would have practically killed for, so I felt terribly guilty when I realized within just a couple of weeks that I hated it."

"How come?"

"I'm not sure exactly. But it had something to do with not wanting to be stuck in an office or forced to adhere to the same schedule day in and day out. I was also impatient

72

about the length of time it would take before I'd have any chance at a writing assignment. So, while I still had my job, I did a couple of articles that sold to some of the specialty magazines. Nothing spectacular, but enough to encourage me to go out on my own."

"And the rest is history?"

Jenny smiled broadly. She sensed he understood her drive for independence better than most people ever would. In that, at least, they were two of a kind. "I guess you could say that. Anyway, I've never looked back."

That's pretty close to my own philosophy. Only in my case, it's never look down."

"I should have remembered that today," Jenny said softly. "Then maybe I wouldn't have slipped."

As she spoke she wondered if Logan would recognize her attempt to explain what had happened to her during the climb as an apology for her behavior afterward. To her great relief, he did.

Reaching across the table, he touched her hand gently. "Is that what went wrong? You slipped?"

"Yes, you were right about my not wanting to remember. But I'm sure now that my left foot wasn't properly placed. It knocked my balance off and I fell." Her eyes darkened as she relived that terrifying moment.

"Don't think about it anymore," Logan instructed her. "You remembered, so next time you'll know what to watch out for. But there's no reason to dwell on it."

Jenny agreed. She was only too willing to allow herself to be distracted by him. It was far more pleasant to concentrate on his strength and gentleness, on the intelligence and sensitivity that shone in everything he did, on the tingling currents of anticipation he unleashed within her.

"Would you like to order now?" the waiter inquired softly, unsure whether the couple who was so caught up in each other would hear him.

73

It took a moment, but his question finally penetrated. With difficulty they managed to turn their attention to the menus long enough to decide that they both liked chateaubriand, endive salad, and crisp shoestring potatoes.

Consulting the wine list, Logan asked, "What do you think of a '78 Stag's Leap Burgundy?"

The products of that particular California vineyard were among Jenny's favorites, as she quickly told him. When the bottle was brought, Logan insisted on their both tasting it before he nodded his approval to the sommelier. His tacit acknowledgment that her palate was the equal of his own might seem a small courtesy to some, but Jenny was touched by it. She liked the fact that this big, hard man who didn't hesitate to pit himself against the most awesome forces of nature was still capable of showing such innate consideration.

That sense of him as someone very special continued to grow in her through the excellent dinner that followed. The conversation between them never lagged. It seemed as though they had no end of things to talk about, from their childhoods to their feelings about recent news events, books they had both read, movies each wanted to see. They smiled often and laughed easily, without ever being aware of the occasionally indulgent looks cast their way by the restaurant staff and other diners who could not help but notice the distinctly romantic glow surrounding their table.

They lingered so long over dinner that by the time they became aware of the late hour, the rest of the tables were empty. Settling the check, Logan apologized to the waiter for delaying his departure, but the man brushed that aside with good humor that seemed to owe nothing to the sizable tip. He and the maître d' were both smiling benignly as they bowed the couple out.

"I had no idea it was so late," Jenny admitted when they were once again settled in the jeep.

"Neither did I." Glancing over at her, Logan asked softly, "Are you tired?"

Silently, she shook her head. She didn't want the evening to end and neither, it seemed, did Logan.

"How about coming back to my place for a brandy?"

Jenny hesitated only a moment. If she agreed, she really wouldn't be committing herself to anything but a drink and another hour or two in his company. "All right."

The cedar shingle and stone house that had looked so impressive from the outside was even more so once seen from the interior. Almost the entire first floor was taken up by a spacious living area dominated by a large, circular fireplace placed at the center of the room. Around it, natural-cotton seating units and lush Oriental rugs shone against the highly polished wood floor. A low wall doubled as a counter in front of the well-equipped kitchen. In the far corner, an open staircase led up to the sleeping loft on which a wide platform bed was just visible.

Jenny scrupulously averted her eyes from that part of the house. Kicking off her shoes, she settled down near the fire. Logan joined her there, having shed his jacket and tie. He handed her a crystal goblet containing several inches of fragrant brandy.

"You have a beautiful home," she said softly. "Was it here when you bought the land for the school, or did you build it?"

"I built it, but not in the way you probably mean. While the architect and contractors were working on the school, I put this place up myself."

"Where had you learned to do that?"

"I hadn't. But I'd always wanted to build my own house. So I learned as I went along." Logan laughed ruefully. "I suppose the men I'd hired could have built half a dozen houses in the time it took me to do this one. But I was less concerned with actually getting it finished than with just doing it. If that makes any sense?"

It did to Jenny. She admired him even more for not being afraid to tackle something at which he might fail. Although, when she thought about it, she had to admit it was difficult to imagine Logan not being successful at anything he tried. Some goals might take him longer than others, but sooner or later she suspected he would get to exactly where he wanted to be.

Which brought her to the fact that he had just taken the brandy snifter from her hand, set it down next to his own on the flagstones around the fireplace, and drawn her gently but firmly into his arms.

"You smell good," he murmured into her hair.

"That's my perfume, *Vent de Nuit.* It's my favorite. I bought it in . . ."

His lips, touching lightly against hers, cut off her nervous chatter. "Relax, Jenny. I just want to kiss you."

She could handle that, couldn't she? After all, she was a grown woman who had been kissed hundreds of times. It was no big deal.

Maybe she was wrong about that. . . . The way Logan kissed . . . Maybe it was a very big deal indeed.

"You're so soft," he murmured thickly, "and so sweet. Kiss me back, Jenny. There's so much passion in you. Let me feel it."

His gentle urging was enough to snap her last thin hold on restraint. Without allowing herself to think about what she was doing, she let him know the full extent of her desire.

A low groan broke from him. Powerful arms closed around her, lowering her to the thickly carpeted floor. His warm, searching mouth wreaked havoc along the delicate line of her throat and the pearly smoothness of her shoul-

76

ders revealed by the low-cut dress. His hands ran over her back, caressing the soft curve of her buttocks before coming around to cup her breasts. Lean, hard fingers stroked over her nipples, which thrust taut and aching through the thin material.

"Logan . . . please . . ."

"Please what, Jenny? Tell me. That's all I want, to please you and be pleased."

"I—I want . . . Oh, Logan!" Waves of delight washed over her, following the path of his hands and mouth. He was so gentle, so understanding of her every need and wish. He felt so good against her, and she had come to care for him so much.

A soft sigh escaped her as she gave up the battle with herself. "Don't stop, Logan," she moaned. "Please, just don't stop."

His growl of purely male satisfaction reverberated deep within her. Standing, he lifted her effortlessly, cradling her slender body high against his chest as he took the steps two at a time.

In the bedroom, nestled under the eaves, he set her down gently. Without her shoes she came barely to his shoulders. The sheer size and strength of him made her breath catch in her throat. On tiptoe, she reached up to touch trembling fingers to the first of the buttons still fastened on his shirt.

"You're so beautiful," she breathed. "I never thought of a man as being beautiful before. But you are."

Logan shook his head, his eyes molten silver in the shadowy light. "No, you're the one who is beautiful. Exquisitely so. I can hardly believe it."

Though she could sense the almost uncontrollable urgency in him, he still managed to stand quietly as she slowly unfastened each of the buttons and eased the shirt from his shoulders. The massive expanse of bronze skin stretched tautly over muscle and sinew made her breath catch. Not even when she saw him in the sauna had she been so affected by his body. She couldn't even say he was everything she had ever dreamed of, because her imaginings had simply never gotten that close to perfection.

So caught up was she in the impact of his nearness that she barely felt him unzipping the dress at her back. Only when it fell away, to reveal her in nothing more than a lacy bra and panties, and her panty hose, did she shiver slightly.

"Are you cold?" Logan muttered huskily, making short work of her stockings. The touch of his fingers down the length of her legs increased her trembling.

"No, not cold . . ." Her mouth brushed across his chest, savoring the faintly salty tang of his skin. He smelled of soap and sandalwood aftershave and an essentially male scent that excited her tremendously. Her small hands drifted to the buckle of his belt even as he unhooked the front clasp of her bra.

The flare of passion in his slate-gray eyes delighted her. She moaned as he bent his head to first nuzzle the ivory mounds of her breasts, then gently lick and suckle her aching nipples. Rivulets of pleasure surged through her. Grasping the tight curls of silvery hair lying against his scalp, she pressed him closer.

She felt the deep tremor that ran through him as his big hands slid into her panties, stroking and kneading the soft flesh he found until she whimpered in need. Helplessly, she arched against him. A gasp broke from her as she felt the proof of his own desire rising hard and urgent against the sensitive skin of her abdomen.

His big hand moved again, drawing moans of pleasure from her. Beneath the increasingly fierce demand of his touch, the thin silk of her panties tore.

"Sorry," he muttered thickly into her mouth.

"Doesn't matter." Nothing did, except that he go on making her feel the rippling currents of mounting pressure that were coiling one upon the other deep within her.

Gently, he urged her backward. She felt the edge of bed against her knees in the instant before he let her drop across it. Lying on the dark sheets, she looked up at him, watching as he swiftly stripped off the rest of his clothes.

Far in the back of her mind, a tiny quiver of fear sprang to life as she stared at the full power of his masculinity revealed to her. But it vanished instantly as Logan came down beside her on the bed.

Despite what was clearly his intense arousal, he showed no desire to hurry her in any way. Every movement, every touch, was slow and gentle. Lying beside her, he smiled reassuringly as he brushed a stray wisp of hair from her brow. His hand trailed lightly down her cheek to cup her chin. Bending forward, he barely touched his lips to hers, teasing her with gossamer kisses that made her ache for more. His tongue leisurely followed the inner curve of her lips before at last meeting hers in a loving duel.

"Jenny . . . you're so beautiful," he moaned as she moved against him, her breasts brushing the hair-rough skin of his chest.

"N-no, you're the one whose beautiful . . . so strong and ˉo . . . tender . . ."

It was the tenderness that stunned her. Not for a moment had she thought Logan would be rough, but she had not expected him to show such extraordinary understanding of her needs and wishes. Though this was their first time together, it was almost as though they had been lovers for years, so sensitive was he to her every response.

As his mouth moved along the slender column of her neck to nestle in the hollow at the base of her throat, his hands stroked her back delicately before applying just the right degree of pressure in slow circular motions between her shoulder blades. A pleased laugh broke from Logan as he saw how delicious this made her feel.

"I knew it," he murmured huskily, nuzzling the curve of her breasts. "The back is a highly underrated erogenous zone."

Jenny gasped as his neatly trimmed nails scratched lightly along her spine, evoking shivering waves of delight. Anxious as much to give as receive pleasure, she let her own hands wander down the sinewy stretch of his back to caress the hard, lean ridge of his hips.

The tremor that rippled through him was her reward. He moved slightly, enough so that she could continue her exploration along the sculpted muscles of his chest. As she followed the thick mat of golden hair down across his taut abdomen, Logan groaned. The silken curls clinging to his well-shaped head teased her skin as his mouth traced all the way around the lush curve of her breast before his tongue at last flicked out to taste the swollen bud ripe for his touch.

As he drew her nipple within the warm, moist cavern of his mouth to suckle her gently, she began to tremble. By the time his big hands moved over her again, seeking the ultrasensitive skin of her inner thighs, she could not stop. Low whimpers of need tore from her.

"L-Logan . . . please . . ."

He hesitated only a moment longer, heightening her pleasure to almost painful intensity before at last bringing them together. Entering her slowly and carefully, he waited until her hips arched instinctively to meet him. Only then did he thrust fully within her, bringing them both to explosive release.

Afterward, Jenny lay warm and soft in his arms, savoring the languid afterglow of their love. She had no regrets. A month ago, the idea that she could so wantonly yield herself to a man she had only known a few weeks would have been unthinkable. But some secret, hidden part of her seemed to have known Logan forever. He was the one man her woman's soul was utterly attuned to. For her at least, their lovemaking had been a vow echoed by every cell of her being. Heart, mind, and body, she was convinced she belonged with Logan.

She fell asleep wondering if there was any chance he might feel the same way about her.

CHAPTER SIX

The smell of coffee woke her. She stirred hesitantly, reluctant to emerge from a sleep deeper and more restful than any she had ever experienced before. Only gradually did she become aware of her surroundings. When the realization of where she was at last reached her, she sat up quickly, holding the sheet over her breasts and glancing around warily.

Logan was nowhere in sight, which was just as well, considering the flush that stained her cheeks at the mere thought of him. Jenny shook her head dazedly, hardly daring to credit her memories of the passion-filled night they had shared.

Over and over he had drawn her to him, bringing her repeatedly to fulfillment so complete that she thought each time nothing could possibly surpass it, only to discover a short while longer that she was wrong. In his arms she became a wild thing freed of all restraint, driven solely by the need to give herself completely and in the process to take everything he so ardently offered.

Nor was Logan the only one to initiate their lovemaking. Waking in the darkness, she had instinctively reached out to him, tracing patterns of delight along the hard, sinewy length of his body, enraptured by his unbridled response that amplified her own.

In the fresh light of morning she could only marvel at

her wantonness. A secret, womanly smile curved her love-bruised mouth as she looked back on the magical hours of the night. Whatever happened, at least she would always have their precious memory.

She was about to climb out of bed when the sound of footsteps on the stairs to the loft sent her scrambling back under the covers. She barely made it before Logan appeared carrying a tray, his sun-washed curls still damp from a shower and his long, lean body clad in a white turtleneck sweater and gray slacks.

A warm smile reminiscent of the intimacy they had shared lit his eyes as he saw she was awake. Putting the tray down on a low table near the bed, he sat down next to her, his bronze hand gently brushing back the tumult of coffee-dark curls falling over her forehead.

"Good morning," he said gently.

Self-conscious though she was under his slow, knowing scrutiny, Jenny could not look away. Her gaze met his as she murmured, "Good morning."

"Did you sleep well?" he inquired with good-humored courtesy, well aware of the effect his nearness was having on her.

Stirring restively under his hand, she nodded. "Yes, but I really should get up now." She had no idea of the time, but the bright light streaming in through the windows beneath the eaves told her it must be at least a few hours after dawn. Soon the rest of the students and instructors would be stirring, if they weren't already.

The problem of what to do about her clothes darted through her mind. She could hardly hope to make her way inconspicuously back to her cabin clad in an evening dress and high heels.

Fortunately, it seemed that Logan had already thought of that and taken steps to forestall her embarrassment. As he handed her a steaming mug of coffee, he said, "I hope you don't mind, but I went over to your cabin this morning and picked up a few things I thought you'd want." He gestured toward a neat pile at the foot of the bed. A teasing gleam entered his eyes as he added, "I took the ones you wore yesterday back with me, or at least all of them that were still wearable."

Not for the first time, Jenny wished she possessed a far greater degree of sophistication in her dealings with men. A more experienced woman would undoubtedly have laughed off his none-too-subtle reminder of their unbridled passion. But she managed only to blush, to Logan's obvious amusement. He laughed warmly even as he apparently decided to take mercy on her.

"I'll leave you to get dressed. When you're ready, come downstairs and we'll have breakfast."

She waited until he vanished back down the steps before making her way to the bathroom. Casting a wistful look at the huge whirlpool bath, she settled for a hot shower under pulsating jets of water set on either side of the marble enclosure. A heated towel rack yielded a huge length of thick terry cloth that enveloped her slenderness. Wiping off the mirror, she gazed at her own image in mingled amazement and satisfaction. Her cornflower-blue eyes glowed warmly, her skin was radiant, and every inch of her body seemed to exude an aura of intense fulfillment that could have only one source.

Logan was a magnificent lover, she admitted to herself as she pulled on her clothes. Tender, sensitive, forceful without ever being in the least cruel, and with a hint of vulnerability that touched some hidden wellspring of her femininity.

He was also, she admitted a bit ruefully as she became aware for the first time of what he had selected for her, extremely thorough and practical. Besides heavy wool pants and a warm sweater, he had also found her climbing boots, thick socks, underwear, her brush and comb, and her makeup bag. Not even the daily vitamin she took had been forgotten. One was nestled in a folded-over tissue next to the moisturizer she used to protect her skin from the wind and sun.

Swallowing it, she grimaced in the mirror. For a cool, level-headed professional who ran her life as efficiently as she did her business, she was showing a hitherto unsuspected capacity for infatuation. Or at least that was how she chose to characterize her feelings for Logan. He captivated and beguiled her, thrilled and fascinated her. He made her feel better about herself and the world in general than she ever had in her life. He filled her with tender yearnings she had never before experienced. If that was love, she wasn't ready to admit it yet.

She went downstairs to find him busy at the stove, scrambling eggs to go with the rashers of crisp bacon and toasted muffins that waited on warming plates. He glanced up at her cheerfully. "Help yourself to more coffee, if you want it. There's orange juice in the fridge."

He was so matter-of-fact that Jenny felt vaguely annoyed. They might have spent the night in separate rooms for all the interest he was showing. Not until she sat down across the table from him did she realize he was watching her rather warily.

As she bit into a muffin, he said, "Jenny, you're not sorry about last night, are you?"

Swallowing hastily, she forced herself to meet his eyes. He looked so uncertain that her throat tightened. It never occurred to her to answer him other than honestly.

"No, Logan, I don't regret it. It was the most beautiful night of my life."

The relief and elation that swept through him were unmistakable. She could almost see the tension leave his powerful body as he visibly relaxed. "That's good," he murmured. "I want you to know I feel the same way."

That surprised her. Did the hours they had shared really mean so much to him? She could hardly dare to believe that was possible. After all, he was far more experienced than she, and must have had many such encounters.

The thought of Logan with other women twisted through her painfully. It was agonizing enough to imagine him with someone else in the past, but the idea that he would have such relationships in the future was unendurable. She took a deep breath, forcing it from her mind. Not in time, though, to keep him from realizing something was wrong.

Concerned, he reached out across the table to take her hand. "Jenny, what's the matter?"

"Nothing."

In a forced attempt at lightness, he teased her gently. "Don't you like my cooking?"

"It's not that. I'm just . . . confused."

"About us?"

Miserably, she nodded. "I guess."

"From what you said a moment ago, I thought you knew how you felt."

"I do. It's . . . your feelings . . ." Afraid to reveal too much, she broke off, staring down at her plate.

Logan didn't respond right away. She could feel his eyes on her for long moments before he finally asked, "Didn't you believe me when I said I felt the same way?"

Jenny hesitated, not knowing what to say. How could she explain to him that she was less concerned about how he viewed what had already happened between them and far more worried about what he envisioned for them in the future? Wishing she had a better grasp of the etiquette of mornings after, she murmured, "I'm not trying to put you on the spot, Logan. Honestly. I'm glad last night meant so much to you."

Silence again, but only for a moment, before everything she had suspected about his intelligence and sensitivity was vividly reaffirmed. "Now I understand," Logan murmured. His hand tightened gently on hers. "Jenny, as far as I'm concerned, last night was only the beginning. Something extraordinary is happening between us. I hope we both want to give it every chance to continue growing."

The smile that lit Jenny's face found its own response in his. He laughed tenderly, regarding her so intently that little shivers of pleasure ran down her spine.

Logan must have felt the same, for he shook his head ruefully. "We've got a class starting in half an hour. Finish your breakfast."

Jenny happily did as he said. She found her appetite was far better than she had thought, and managed to do full justice to his cooking, reassured by the knowledge that she would undoubtedly work off the calories during the morning's lesson.

Helping him stack the plates in the dishwasher, she asked, "Will we be doing the same climb as yesterday?"

"Pretty much, but with a few extras thrown in."

Her mock groan made him laugh. They were still smiling as they walked down to the clearing to meet the rest of the climbing party. If anyone noticed the intimate mood between them, they made no comment. Only Deke grinned as he glanced from one to the other. Jenny didn't doubt for a moment that the young instructor was convinced he knew what had happened. But she kept her expression scrupulously blank as Logan began to explain the day's exercise.

"In addition to the free climbing techniques you practiced yesterday, we're going to be working on some direct-aid methods that can help you if you ever find yourself in a tight spot you have to get out of in a hurry."

Holding up a sample piton and hammer, he went on. "Climbing with the help of devices like this used to be a lot more popular than it is now. So many people relied on these tools that the best-known rock faces and mountains were left scarred by literally thousands of these metal spikes. Nowadays, when we do use them at all, it's with a great deal of care. Besides being cautious about where we put them, all pitons are removed as we go along.   thing is left behind to mar the natural challenge and beauty of the climb for those who come after. Depending on how much climbing you do, you may never need to rely on them. But just in case you ever do find yourself in a situation you can't get out of in any other way, you need to be thoroughly experienced in their placement and use."

As Logan and the other instructors distributed the pitons and hammers to the students, Jenny glanced up at the peak above them. She was surprised to discover that despite her experience of the previous day, she felt no hesitation about climbing again. The knowledge that Logan would be with her dispelled the fear she would otherwise have felt. After the night they had shared it was impossible not to trust him absolutely.

They started out along the same approach they had used before. Climbing right behind Logan, Jenny found she had no difficulty following and even anticipating his instructions. The only problem she encountered was that her acute awareness of him made it a little hard to concentrate on exactly what she was doing. Several times he had to repeat himself. She could feel him becoming increasingly annoyed, but try though she did, she couldn't bring her unruly emotions under control. Twice more she made elemental mistakes that had Logan snapping at her angrily. Finally to her dismay he said, "This just isn't working out. I should have known better than to climb with you today."

Before she could respond, he called down to the team directly below them. "Deke, come up here. We're switching students."

Jenny had no choice but to comply. Fighting to hide her embarrassment and hurt, she exchanged anchoring ropes with the young ad executive who had been partnering Deke. Logan spoke with the man briefly, assuring that the switch hadn't thrown off his concentration. Without another word to Jenny, he resumed the ascent, leaving her staring after him.

"Come on, now," Deke said softly when they were alone on the ledge. "If you keep looking like that, you'll hurt my feelings. Surely having to climb with me isn't such a disaster?"

His gentle tone and the understanding look in his hazel eyes were almost her undoing. Swallowing hard, she murmured, "No, of course not. I was just . . . surprised. That's all."

Checking to make sure the rope was properly tied around her waist, Deke nodded. "Yeah, life has a way of doing that to you. Now, what say we get on with this clambake?"

Smiling just a bit damply, Jenny agreed. Her enjoyment in the climb was gone. She just wanted to get it over with as quickly as possible.

For the next hour she followed Deke's instructions meticulously as he explained how to select the best piton for different types of cracks, how to be sure it was securely pounded in, and how to remove it so as to leave the rock face unscarred.

Occasionally, she caught sight of Logan and his student up ahead, but she rigorously ignored them. With her concentration focused utterly on the task at hand, she made no further mistakes, nor did she have any energy left over to be more than remotely conscious of the steep fall beneath her. Without even being aware of it, she climbed with steady grace, making progress so rapidly that even Deke was impressed.

"You've really caught on to this," he said as they rested briefly on a ledge. "Are you sure you've never done it before?"

"Never before and quite probably never again," Jenny informed him. "Once the research for this article is done, I'm staying off mountains."

"Oh?" he murmured noncommittally. "Why's that?"

"Because . . . because I've got better things to do, that's why."

Deke laughed. Gently, he said, "Wrong answer, Jenny. You can say a lot of things about climbing, but you can't claim it's dull. I'd have to be deaf, dumb, and blind not to know you're as far from bored than you can get. Of course," he added archly, "that doesn't mean you wouldn't rather be doing something else. But frankly, no matter how good a climber you become, certain activities will always be impossible up here."

Taking his meaning all too clearly, Jenny glared at him. But Deke remained imperturbable. He merely laughed as they rose to begin the descent. The first stage went well. Although the downward angle was very steep, Jenny had no difficulty keeping her balance. Her only concern came when it was her turn to anchor Deke so that he could swing out across a chasm. She was worried that her weight and skill wouldn't be up to the task, but he assured her calmly that he had no doubt she could handle it.

Since he was literally betting his life that such was the case, Jenny felt compelled to believe him. Nonetheless, she was hardly breathing as she took up her position against a large rock outcropping, dug her feet into the ground, and got a firm grip on the belaying rope. Her heart skipped a beat as he reached out across several feet of space to find a firm hold perilous feet away. Not until he was safely on the other side did her pulse return to normal.

After that it was easy to follow him. She completed the maneuver without even breathing hard. Deke shook his head admiringly. He was about to compliment her on her newly acquired skill, when a sudden fall of rocks alerted them to the fact that something was wrong below.

Jenny glanced down, only to have her heart rush into her throat as horror surged through her. In the act of completing a similar belaying maneuver, Logan's partner had lost his footing. Feeling his balance go, he had panicked. Instead of reeling in the slake on the rope, he had dropped it. Caught in mid-step between one side of a rock cut and the other, Logan plummeted. He careened off the edge of the cliff, his body thumping heavily against the sharp stones.

The scream that bubbled in Jenny's throat was never released. Almost in the same instant that she realized what was happening, icy calm slammed down over her. Without needing any guidance from Deke, she moved quickly and effectively to help him reach the ledge in the shortest possible time.

In the next few minutes she received a lesson in rescue techniques she could cheerfully have done without. At no time did Deke violate fundamental rules regarding his safety or hers, but he cut every possible corner, took every possible chance to get to the scene of the accident swiftly. As the ad executive blubbered his apologies and excuses, Deke ripped the belaying rope from him and secured it to his own waist. Once it was in place, he gave Jenny terse instructions to help him reel Logan up.

Not until his head appeared over the edge of the rock face, and she realized he was conscious, did some small measure of her anguish ease. Even so, she was trembling as Deke helped him onto the ledge, looking him over quickly for the more visible signs of injury.

"I'm fine," Logan insisted. He glanced up, meeting the younger man's eyes. A quiet word of thanks passed between them. Deke shrugged it off.

"You would have done the same for me," he pointed out, "and probably a lot more efficiently."

"Oh, I don't know," Logan protested lightly. "Seems to me you got here pretty fast."

"I had help." With attention focused on her, Jenny flushed. She didn't want Logan's gratitude or approval. She didn't want anything except to see him get safely off the mountain.

"Shouldn't we start back down?" she asked softly. "We're holding up the rest of the teams."

Logan regarded her for a moment before abruptly nodding. The remainder of the descent was made in silence. When they reached the bottom, Logan went at once to his office with the ad executive. Jenny knew the man would get a fair hearing, but unless he could leave absolutely no doubt that there would be no further repetition of the incident, he would be told to leave the school.

Turning toward her cabin, she hesitated. Logan hadn't asked her to wait for him, hadn't given any indication that he wanted to be with her. But she couldn't just go off as though nothing had happened. If the events of the night before had not been enough to convince her of how much he meant to her, the accident on the mountain had. What it came down to was that her need for him outweighed any other consideration. Squaring her slender shoulders, she decided to take the risk that he might be angered by her presumption.

Letting herself into his house, she went upstairs and switched on the faucets in the whirlpool bath. As it was

92

filling, she turned down the bed and glanced around to see if she might find any pajamas. She didn't. Logan apparently considered them another of civilization's needless trappings. When the tub was ready, she closed the door to keep it warm before going down to the kitchen to mix a hot toddy.

Logan arrived just as she was adding the last touches to the hot buttered rum. He stood for a moment in the door, looking at her. His expression was unreadable. She had no idea whether he was glad or not to see her there.

Taking a deep breath, she forced herself to speak calmly. "I've run you a hot bath. You should get in it before it starts to cool."

He turned away for a moment to shut and lock the door. When he faced her again, Jenny's pulse skipped a beat. The inscrutable look was gone, replaced by an utterly male smile that warmed her all the way through.

"I'll do that," he said softly, "but only if you'll join me."

CHAPTER SEVEN

The sight of the bruises on his back and legs made Jenny flinch. The force of his fall had knocked him against the rock face so hard that not even his heavy clothing had protected him. His bronze skin was broken in places and black-and-blue marks were already forming.

As his clothes fell away, she touched him gingerly. "Are you sure you aren't more seriously hurt than you think?"

"I'm sure," Logan muttered absently, busy pulling her sweater over her head and unzipping her slacks. When she was as naked as he, he stepped into the tub with her. Together they sank into the blissfully hot water.

"You do have good ideas," he told her as he stretched out full length, sipping the buttered rum and letting the swirling jets of water pound against his aching limbs.

"I'm glad you think so. Downstairs I wasn't sure you were glad to see me here."

Logan opened one eye, regarding her through the steamy air. "I was surprised," he admitted. "All the way back from the office I was hoping you'd be here. I just didn't let myself count on it in case I ended up being disappointed."

"And if I hadn't been waiting . . . ?"

"I would have come and gotten you," he told her flatly. A sinewy arm reached out to pull her closer. "What are you doing all the way over there, woman? I thought the idea of this was to make me feel better."

"Oh, but it will," she assured him teasingly. "If you'll just lie back and relax. Forget I'm here."

"Fat chance," Logan muttered. His hands were already slipping down to cup her breasts, his legs entwining with hers. As his mouth moved along the silken line of her throat, Jenny moaned softly. It was impossible to disguise her need for him.

A need that, to her astonishment, he fully returned. She gasped as the hardness of his manhood brushed against her thigh. His intense arousal coming so soon after the almost deadly accident stunned her.

"H-how can you . . . ?" she murmured thickly, dazed by his gentle assault on her senses. "Wouldn't it be better for you to . . . rest?"

"Only if you want me to die of frustration." Shifting slightly in the water, he looked down at her tenderly. "Why so surprised, Jenny? I'm damn glad to be alive. I'd just like to do a little celebrating, that's all."

Oh, well, if that was all . . .

Long moments later she reflected that Logan's idea of a celebration was enough to drown most men. With nearly intolerable skill and patience, he brought her to a level of ecstasy that was so intense as to be almost painful.

His mouth traced a fiery line from the delicate curve of her brow down along her flushed cheeks to the hollow at the base of her throat. Teasing her with feather-light kisses, he stroked the silken length of her back to the dimples at the arch of her buttocks and beyond. When she moaned helplessly, he relented just a bit. Big hands slid along her gently curved hips to the narrow incline of her waist and the swelling breasts that ached for his caress.

Beneath the faintly rough touch of his callused fingers, Jenny heard herself moan again. She loved what he was doing to her . . . how he was making her feel . . . what her own hands and mouth were discovering as she explored him in turn.

Despite the enervating heat of the whirlpool, his ardor seemed without limit. She had reached almost intolerable limits of pleasure when he at last drew her upward until she sat straddling his lap before lowering her carefully, inch by exquisite inch onto him.

When he was fully within her, his hands slid down her sides to grasp her hips. "Lean back, Jenny," he coaxed her hoarsely. She obeyed unhesitantly, trusting him to keep her head above the swirling water that pounded over them both.

As he shifted her slightly, pulsating jets of foam struck against both her nipples. She groaned in delight, vividly aware of the thrusting hardness moving deeper and deeper inside her. Matching the jets' surging rhythm, Logan brought her closer and closer to the edge of dazzling fulfillment. She bore it as long as she could, until at last a keening moan broke from her.

Only then did he give in to his own driving need. Carrying her from the tub, rivulets of water streaming off them, he laid her flat on the thick fur rug, and lowered himself on top of her. Jenny opened her legs to him joyfully, desperate for the feel of him inside her again. This time there was no gentleness in his possession. He drove into her fiercely, moaning his pleasure into her mouth. They crested together within seconds, and lay spent and panting on the floor for long moments before either could stir.

When she was finally able to talk again, she murmured shakily, "I'm not sure this is the best possible treatment for those bruises. What do you say we get into bed?"

Logan chuckled softly. He propped himself up on an elbow, staring down at her radiant features. "I'm game to try it, if you are."

Laughing, they dried each other and, leaning together in a tangle of arms and legs, just managed to make it to the bed before collapsing on it. As his head hit the pillow, he murmured softly, "Jenny, forgive me, but I'm about to do something terrible." Seconds later he was fast asleep, leaving her staring at him in tender sympathy.

Her eyes drifted over him slowly, drinking in the sight of tousled hair lying like curls of silver against the dark pillow, sun-washed lashes thick against his high cheekbones. The sculpted planes and hollows of his face were relaxed in sleep, his sensual lips parted slightly as he breathed deeply.

She sighed contentedly, letting her gaze wander down the strong column of his throat, over massive shoulders and powerful, hair-rough chest to the tapering line of his waist and hips merging into sinewy legs. He was so magnificently male that he took her breath away. But he was also, she realized as she studied him, more badly hurt than he had cared to admit.

The abrasions on his arms and torso were raw and jagged, and the bruises decorating a good portion of the rest of him were already turning purple. Rising quickly, she padded back into the bathroom. In the cabinet she found a tube of antiseptic cream. Returning to the bed, she knelt down beside him. Carefully, so as not to disturb his sleep, she gently rubbed the cream into the worst of his injuries. Logan sighed once or twice under her tender touch, but did not wake.

Satisfied that she had done everything she could, Jenny pulled the covers over him before sliding into the bed at his side. For a long time she lay awake, watching him in the fading light. It occurred to her that they would both be missed at dinner, but she could not worry about that. All that mattered was that he was safe and she was with him. Nestling closer to his long, hard body, she closed her eyes, thinking she would just rest for a while. But she hadn't counted on the effect of relief more profound than any she had ever known. Within minutes she, too, was fast asleep.

Logan woke deep in the night to the sound of terrified sobbing. Bewildered, he turned over and instinctively gathered Jenny into his arms. Not until he was holding her did he realize the sobs were her own and that she was clearly trapped in a nightmare.

"Wake up, sweetheart," he murmured gently. "It's just a dream. Wake up."

Surfacing through waves of terror, she held on to his voice as to a lifeline. By the time she at last fought her way back to consciousness, her body was damp with perspiration and she was shaking violently.

"L-Logan," she murmured brokenly, "that dream . . . so horrible . . ."

"Shhh, it's all over. Nothing to be scared about." Still only half awake himself, he was nonetheless acutely aware of the depth of her fright.

Holding her closer, he gently stroked her hair and back, crooning to her softly until the tension left her body. Tilting her head back, he looked down at her tenderly. "Better now?"

Mutely, Jenny nodded. She did feel better, but she couldn't bring herself to tell him why. Just the sight of him next to her, the feel of his skin against her own, the low, reassuring murmur of his voice, went a long way toward banishing the hideous image of him falling off the side of the cliff to his death on the jagged rocks below. The vision had been so compellingly real that even nestled in his arms she was hard-pressed to shake it off.

Though she was exhausted by the emotional strain of an experience that seemed only too real, she was reluctant to go back to sleep again and risk having the dream return. Moreover, she was hungry.

As her stomach growled indelicately, Logan laughed. "We did skip dinner, didn't we?"

"Mmmm . . . we were preoccupied."

"I'll say. I can't remember ever being so delightedly . . . preoccupied before in my life."

"I'm glad to hear it," Jenny observed wryly. "I'd hate to think you carried on like that all the time."

"Hardly," Logan admitted, "or I would never have made it to the grand old age of thirty-five." Rubbing his stomach, he added, "And if I'm going to make it much further, I've got to get something to eat. How about raiding the refrigerator?"

Jenny agreed at once. Wrapped in one of his terry-cloth robes that all but swallowed her slender frame, she went downstairs with him. In the back of her mind she had presumed mountain climbers subsisted on a diet of alfalfa sprouts and tofu, and it was true that Logan's refrigerator was stocked with a wide variety of healthful foods. But her eye fell on something far better suited to late-night snacking.

"*Brownies*? You like Sara Lee brownies?"

"Only every once in a while," he said sheepishly.

"Then you've got more self-control than I do. I could eat them every day." Reaching for the milk, she added, "I don't, of course. But tonight I think I'll make an exception."

Back in bed, they curled up under the covers and fed each other bites of the rich chocolate confection.

"Glutton," Logan murmured teasingly as she took a particularly large nibble from the slice he held.

"You bet. Better hurry or they'll all be gone."

Heeding the warning, he made short work of his share. Watching him, Jenny giggled. "I'll bet when you were little and had a birthday, you always snuck an extra piece of the cake to take to bed."

His eyes widened slightly. "How did you know that?"

"Because I did the same thing. The absolutely best times to eat something this decadent is either late at night or first thing in the morning for breakfast."

"Are you warning me you're the type who keeps the bed full of crumbs?"

"Yep. But don't worry. I promise not to brush them over to your side."

Grinning, she began to lick the last of the icing from her fingers only to have Logan take her hand and insist on finishing the job.

One thing led to another, and before long they were once again entwined together, making slow, languorous love that brought them both to an explosive height from which they drifted naturally back into sleep.

By morning the nightmare that had awakened her in such terror was no more than a faint memory. But even as she dressed and shared breakfast with Logan, she could not completely ignore its lingering remnants.

The nervousness she had felt about his occupation from the moment they met had grown vastly worse. What had begun as simple concern was now full-fledged fear. The thought of Logan being hurt sickened her. The idea that he might be killed was too intolerable even to be considered.

His routine acceptance of danger as part of his life tormented her. Though she still told herself she wasn't sure what she felt was love, her feelings for him—whatever they might be—made her acutely vulnerable. The knowledge that she was no longer complete within herself, but was becoming more and more dependent on someone else for the very essentials of life, haunted her through all that day and the next.

By the following morning the weather had worsened enough to make climbing classes inadvisable. Instead, Logan used the opportunity for a discussion of the techniques learned so far and how they might be applied in different situations.

That led naturally to questions about the various climbs he had made. There was considerable interest from all the students as he talked about his experiences in the Alps, Himalayas, and of course, the Cascades. But it was the ascent he had made in Alaska the previous year that sparked the most excitement.

"You led the team that tried to climb Mount McKinley last summer, didn't you?" one of the students asked.

Logan nodded. His expression was suddenly closed, as though he were withdrawing into himself. But only Jenny seemed to notice his discomfort.

"Did the falls happen near the summit?" another student asked.

"Yes, within several hundred feet."

A memory from her research surfaced in her mind. A picture of Logan standing gaunt and exhausted at the base camp, the gigantic mountain seeming to hang in the sky behind him. Three covered stretchers on the ground. The only remains recovered from the accident that had claimed seven climbers out of a party of twenty. Despite the finest preparations, the greatest skill, and the most meticulous caution, the mountain had still bested them.

Many team leaders would never have attempted to recover any of the bodies, believing the effort futile. But Logan had insisted, and had driven himself to the brink of collapse in his determination to do so. Yet even he had to be satisfied to bring out the three. The others would remain buried forever under the tons of snow and ice that covered the mountain's peak.

The discussion moved on to happier topics, the instructors chiming in with their own stories. Dinner was livelier than ever, as tales of high adventure, extreme challenge, and ultimate victory were traded back and forth. The students, basking in the sense of camaraderie, began to reveal their own hopes. It seemed that everyone except Jenny nurtured a dream of climbing some particular mountain.

Men who a few weeks before had been largely desk-bound were now just beginning to dare hope that lifelong fantasies might actually be fulfilled. They had taken the first big step in coming to the school. With the preparation they received there, it was not impossible that some at least would achieve their dreams. Jenny could admire their courage even as she felt no desire to emulate them.

Her own hopes were far simpler. Looking across the table at Logan, she caught the gleam in his eye and smiled. There was no surprise when a few minutes later he rose to say good night, holding out his hand to her as naturally as if he had always done so. She felt only the slightest embarrassment at having their relationship out in the open, and even that faded as they walked along the path back to his house.

In the quiet darkness, when just a hint of late spring frost touched the air, it seemed utterly natural to be at his side. They talked softly, neither wanting to disturb the tranquility surrounding them. Logan paused once to glance up at the sky. The thick clouds that had hugged the peaks all day were growing even denser. To Jenny, they seemed so close that she would only have to stretch out a hand to touch them.

"The weather's getting worse," Logan murmured.

"Does it matter? Everyone enjoyed today, and got a lot out of it. I'm sure no one would mind if we had to have lessons inside again tomorrow."

"That's not what I'm worried about," he told her gently. "Whenever we get an unexpected storm at this time of year, somebody always seems to get stranded up there."

Turning, he pointed toward the looming mass of the Devil's Summit standing out stark against the sky. The jagged peak looked ominous even by day. By night it appeared so menacing and sinister that she could well understand how it had gotten its name.

She knew Logan had climbed it many times, but was glad nonetheless that it was not part of the beginner's course. Only those who came for advanced training tackled the sheer cliffs, icy chasms, and snow-capped peak that made it a challenge to even the most experienced mountaineers. It seemed incredible to her that a relatively unskilled climber would even consider approaching it, much less during poor weather.

Her disbelief must have shone in her face, for Logan said, "I know it sounds crazy, but it does happen. I just hope this time we'll get lucky and everyone will have the sense to give the Devil plenty of room. At least until the storm blows over."

But that did not prove to be the case. Shortly before dawn, as icy rain splattered against the windows, the telephone beside Logan's bed rang. He picked it up groggily, listened for a moment, and cursed.

Jenny, waking beside him, caught enough of the brief conversation to know something very bad had happened. When he stalked to the closet to get dressed, she sat up, holding the blankets close against the chill, and watching him worriedly.

"What is it?"

"Just what I was afraid of. Two tourists are missing from an inn about a mile from here. The owner presumed they'd gone out to dinner, and went to bed figuring they could let themselves in. He woke up about an hour ago, when rain started coming in one of his windows. Decided

103

he'd better check the place over to make sure there weren't any other leaks. He noticed a room key still at the desk. Woke up the rest of his staff and started asking questions. Seems someone remembered overhearing the guests at breakfast talking about climbing the Devil's Summit. The idiots!"

Glancing out the window lashed by rain and high wind, Jenny's eyes darkened. It would be bad enough to be out in such a storm, but to be trapped on the side of a mountain . . . "You don't really think they're up there?"

Logan shrugged, buckling a heavy utility belt around his taut waist. "It wouldn't be the first time. And if they are, somebody had better find them fast. Otherwise . . ."

He didn't have to finish. No great experience with climbing was needed to understand the deadly potential of sheer wind-swept cliffs and bitterly cold temperatures. If a fall didn't kill them, exposure would. Unless they were rescued swiftly.

The temptation to ask why he had to be the one to go was almost irresistible, but she beat it down, knowing full well how he would respond. There was no more experienced, skillful climber in the area. That alone was enough reason for him to lead the rescue team. But moreover, he would not be the man he was if he could sit safe at home while others were endangered.

Resigned to the fact that she could not stop him, Jenny leaped from the bed. "I'm going with you."

In the act of pulling on a thick sweater, he growled, "The hell you are! You're staying right here."

"I don't mean I want to climb with you," she explained quickly. "I know that's out of the question. But surely there's something else I can do?"

He had already started to shake his head when she

104

added, "Anyway, it doesn't matter whether you agree or not. I'm still going."

"You don't know what you're talking about," he insisted, lacing up his boots. "It'll be bitter cold and soaking wet out there. There'll be no shelter of any kind, even for the support team."

Jerking on her own clothes, Jenny seized on this last part. "So there will be people standing by to help. At the base of the summit, right? Then that's where I'll be."

The mutinous set of her chin warned him that simply trying to forbid her to go wasn't working. More gently, he said, "Try to understand. I don't want to be worrying about you while I'm climbing. I'll have enough on my hands without that."

Jenny didn't want to think about what he would be confronting. She continued to dress as she said, "I've been in far worse situations without getting hurt. Believe me, I can take care of myself."

"Famous last words," Logan muttered, but he gave up the effort to dissuade her. Though he wasn't ready to admit it, he admired her determination and he was secretly glad that when he got back down, as he was confident he would, she would be waiting there for him.

Once outside, it quickly became clear that the weather was even worse than they had thought. Even with the jeep's high beams on, it was almost impossible to see. The wind gusts that struck them over and over were powerful enough to rock the vehicle violently. Followed by other cars carrying the instructors Logan had notified, they inched along the rain-washed roads. The trip seemed to take hours, but in fact only a few minutes passed before they reached the staging area at the base of Devil's Summit.

As Deke and the other young men gathered around Logan to begin planning the ascent, Jenny helped the

105

emergency medical team from a nearby hospital set up a tent and unpack supplies. The police arrived minutes later with a mobile generator, and powerful searchlights were positioned to illuminate the major access routes up the mountain. Despite their high intensity, they did little to penetrate the thick shroud of fog. After the first few hundred feet, Devil's Summit was wrapped in deadly mystery. If anyone was trapped up there, they could not be seen.

Logan and his team listened carefully as a sergeant from the state police questioned the hotel owner. "Before these men start out," he said, gesturing to the climbers, "I want to hear from you one more time whether or not you think those people are actually up there."

"I just don't know," the ashen-faced man groaned. "My busboy heard them talking about making the climb. He's a good kid, smart, reliable. If he knew the area better, he'd have told them not to go. As it is, he just remembered what they said." Wearily, he added, "But just because they talked about it doesn't mean they went. Maybe their car ran off the road somewhere, or they just decided to skip out on their bill. Could be any number of reasons why they're gone."

"Their luggage is still in their room?"

"Yes, that's the first thing I checked after the kid reported what they'd said. I found a book about climbing." He snorted derisively. "A beginner's guide to the sport. Can you believe that?"

"All too easily," Logan muttered. He had heard enough. Turning to his team, he said, "What it comes down to is that those people may or may not be up there. The only way we're going to find out is to go up after them. If they are there and we don't look, they'll be dead within a few hours. That's guaranteed. But if any of you wants to bet this is all a false alarm and skip the climb, I'll understand."

Nobody moved. Logan waited a moment, then abruptly nodded. "All right. Let's get started."

In the ghostly glare of the searchlights, his eyes glittered with silvery fire as they searched for and found Jenny. For just a moment their gazes held. Long enough to say everything for which there were no words. She breathed in deeply, willing herself to look calm. Not for the world would she let him carry away the image of her frightened and tearful. She even managed a slight smile, which apparently reassured him. He rapped out an order, causing the climbing party to form up quickly behind him. All their immense discipline and training was evident as they moved swiftly up the steep incline and were soon lost from sight.

For an hour or so there was enough work to be done around the base camp to keep everyone's mind occupied. More medical supplies were set out to cope with the hypothermia, broken bones, and other injuries that were likely to occur under such conditions. Hot coffee and rolls were brought over from a nearby inn and gratefully received.

The police were in frequent contact with Logan by radio and were able to follow his route on the map of the summit spread out under the tent. He was checking all the most likely places where novice climbers might get stuck and seek shelter, but so far at least he had found no traces of anyone.

The sun rising over the eastern foothills did nothing to dispel the leaden gloom surrounding the area. Icy rain continued to pelt down and the fog showed no sign of lessening.

An hour dragged by and then another. There was serious talk of recalling the search party. Surely, the reasoning went, if there were climbers on the summit, some sign of them would have been found before then. With conditions so difficult, Logan and the other men were becoming weary. But their inclination was to continue. Some sixth sense refined through hundreds of ascents warned that they should not turn back. It was little enough to go on, but they decided to take the chance.

At mid-morning, their tenacity was rewarded. Logan spotted a piton protruding from a crevasse almost halfway up the mountain. Its positioning was amateurish and its appearance indicated it could not have been in place very long. A few minutes later they spotted their quarry. Two bodies, a man's and a woman's, were resting inside a shallow depression cut into the face of the mountain. They had apparently crawled in there seeking protection from the storm.

Deke reported the sighting to the base camp as Logan lowered himself over the side. Anxious moments dragged past before he reported both were still alive, though only marginally.

After that, everything happened very quickly. A fast but comprehensive report on the victims' condition was made to the waiting medical team while rope slings and stretchers were fashioned to enable them to be safely lowered down the precipice. First aid was administered, but it was clear even to those on the ground that far more extensive treatment was required if the man and woman were to have any chance of surviving.

With each moment vital to the life-and-death struggle, the descent had to be made as rapidly as possible. But the fog still shrouding the mountain made every step treacherous. With the agreement of the rest of the team, Logan decided to take the far more difficult west face, whose sheer drops challenged the most seasoned climber but which also afforded a much faster way down, provided nothing went wrong.

Radio contact was broken off as the men concentrated totally on the precarious path they had to follow to safety.

Those on the ground could only wait anxiously, straining for any sight of movement on the summit.

For Jenny, this was the worst time yet. At least when Logan was staying in touch with the support team she could take comfort from the sound of his voice and the knowledge that he was all right. But in the silence following the decision to attempt the west face, her mind filled with a host of terrifying images.

Pacing back and forth outside the tent, heedless of the rain that soaked through her clothes to chill her very bones, her eyes stayed glued to the mountain. Over and over, she told herself that Logan was too capable a climber to attempt a descent he did not think was safe. There was scant reassurance in the words. Too clearly she understood that the slightest misjudgment, the tiniest error, would spell death.

Nor could she even console herself with the thought that he might have turned the point over to Deke or one of the other men. Under such perilous conditions he would never relinquish that responsibility.

It would be Logan who tested each piton and hold, who crossed each ledge and chasm first, who blazed the trail the others would follow. And if he made a mistake, it was unlikely the rest of the team, burdened as it was with two stretchers, would be able to respond in time to save him.

The gnawing pain that had begun in her when she first realized he meant to lead the rescue grew worse with each passing moment. Her head throbbed and her stomach tightened. With her attention so firmly fixed on the mountain, she had difficulty even remembering to breathe.

Time passed with intolerable slowness. She was reluctant to listen to the low conversations going on among the support team in case she heard something that further amplified her fear. But she was unable to stop herself from overhearing when the police sergeant muttered, "Been a while. Think we should try to reestablish contact?"

"I wouldn't," the head of the medical team said. "Last thing they need right now is a distraction."

"Yeah, but I can't say I'm too happy about just sitting here waiting. What if something's gone wrong and now *they* need help?"

"Then," the doctor said succinctly, "we're in a hell of a lot of trouble. Because if Logan Kent can't beat that mountain, no one can. I wouldn't give two cents for anyone else's chances up there."

"So either he gets himself and his team off or they're stuck?"

"That's about the size of it."

The officer whistled softly. "Wonder if he ever wishes he'd just stayed in bed?"

"I would imagine," the doctor muttered, "that thought is occurring to him right about now."

It was easy to see why. The wind, which had been bad enough throughout the rescue attempt, was increasing in force. It whistled round the sharp angles at the base of the summit and pounded against the fir and pine trees that dotted its incline.

The only possible benefit from the violent air currents might have been a lessening of the fog. But instead, it, too, seemed to be getting worse. Even the bottom of the mountain barely yards from where the support team waited was now all but invisible.

Jenny's heart was in her throat, her hands clenched so tightly that the nails dug into her palms. In all the often frightening, dangerous experiences she had lived through as a photojournalist, she had never before come so close to collapsing under the weight of her emotions.

The thought of Logan trapped on the fog-shrouded slope filled her with pure, overwhelming terror. It blotted

110

out all reason, courage, and pride. Even her most basic senses were almost swamped by it. Almost, but not quite.

Through the red cloud of her fear, a tiny sound penetrated, so slight that she thought at first she must have imagined it. No one else moved or gave any indication of having heard. Holding her breath, Jenny leaned forward. Again the sound reached her, this time a bit more distinctly.

Metal jangling against itself. Pitons and hammers attached to a utility belt and striking each other as the wearer moved. The high-pitched sound would travel farther than the low tones of men's voices.

"They're coming!" It didn't matter that her words were thick with unshed tears or that the other members of the support team looked at her doubtfully. Nothing mattered except that the sound was getting closer and that she was running toward it.

CHAPTER EIGHT

"Whoa!" Logan murmured teasingly. "Give me a chance to catch my breath."

"You can breathe later," Jenny insisted, hugging him fiercely. He felt so good, so strong and solid, and above all, so alive. Through the heavy shirt and sweater he wore, she could hear the solid beat of his heart. His arms were wrapped around her, his lips brushing the crown of her head. The whole world was narrowed down to the two of them, standing at the base of the mountain, oblivious to anything or anyone else.

Until Logan managed to get enough of a grip on himself to remember he had a further report for the medical team. When he looked up, they were busy working on the two forms on the stretchers, which, thanks to the first aid they had received, were already beginning to stir.

Catching his glance, Deke smiled. "I told them everything they need to know. We'll take it from here." His engaging grin widened to encompass Jenny, still snug in Logan's embrace. "Looks like you've got your hands full anyway!"

That remained true all the way back to the school as Jenny refused to be parted from him for an instant. Nor did Logan seem disposed to let her go. He kept her close against him as he maneuvered the jeep back along the narrow roads that because of the incessant rain had become little more than mud paths. As soon as they pulled into the parking lot, they were surrounded by anxious students who had some idea of what had happened, but wanted to hear all the details.

Logan obliged them as much as he could in between bites of a substantial breakfast Maggie had prepared for him. As the housekeeper clucked over him, he explained the intricacies of the climb in matter-of-fact terms that still brought home the full danger of the venture.

Despite her empty stomach, Jenny found she could eat nothing. To Maggie's chagrin, she made do with a cup of weak tea, passing up the mounds of blueberry pancakes smothered in maple syrup and accompanied by pan-fried slabs of ham that everyone else attacked with vigor.

They were finishing up when a report came in from the hospital. Despite their ordeal, the man and woman found on the slope would live. It was even likely that they would escape with no permanent reminders of what had happened to them. All their fingers and toes seemed untouched by frostbite and they were emerging from the coma induced by hypothermia without apparent injury.

So far as the doctors were able to determine, they had simply been unaware of the demands of such a climb and had set off believing they would be back at their hotel well before dinner.

When he heard this, Logan shook his head incredulously. He knew that the hotel the tourists were staying at, like every other one in the area, had warnings posted about the dangers of climbing without expert assistance. Maps of the local peaks clearly warned of their perils. As if all this weren't enough, anyone with half an ounce of sense should be able to look at a mountain such as Devil's Summit and know it was unconquerable by any but the most experienced and skilled.

Yet year in and year out, people were trapped on the

slopes. Despite the best efforts of rescue teams, many died. Logan knew perfectly well that this was not the last time he would be called out on such a mercy mission, and despite his irritation with those who brought such calamity down on themselves, he would never refuse to go.

Since the weather remained too poor for outdoor classes, the remainder of the day was devoted to a timely discussion of rescue and first-aid techniques. Jenny had some difficulty putting together the rope slings and stretchers that were essential to any such effort. But she did very well with the medical part. Her penchant for visiting isolated, dangerous spots had long ago made it imperative for her to learn at least the rudiments of emergency treatment. She proved to be every bit as adept as Logan himself at the construction of splints, identification of symptoms, and treatment of the cardiovascular problems that were liable to occur under extreme conditions.

Halfway through the class, he grinned at her admiringly. So softly that only she could hear him, he murmured, "I'd say we make a pretty good team, wouldn't you?"

The blush she was unable to suppress made him chuckle. Throughout the rest of the day she frequently felt his eyes on her, sometimes tenderly, sometimes with a faint note of surprise that puzzled her.

As she was leaving to take a shower and change, Logan caught up with her in the hallway. His silvery gaze fastened on her more intently than ever as he said, "I've asked Maggie to fix dinner for us and send it over to my place. Is that all right with you?"

"Are you sure she doesn't mind? Maggie has a lot of work to do as it is."

"I know," Logan admitted wryly, "and every time I've tried to get her to slow down she's told me to stop sticking my nose into her kitchen. She told me this morning that she wouldn't mind lending a hand."

"Oh. Well, that's fine then. I'll just go change . . ."

His hand on her arm stopped her from leaving. Gently he drew her to him, his lips brushing hers. "Do me a favor, Jenny?"

"All right."

"Wear that blue dress."

Since it was the only dress she had with her she was glad enough to oblige. Back in the cabin she had seen so little of him over the last few days, she showered and changed hurriedly. After the terrible experience of the morning, being apart from Logan even briefly was painful. She needed to be able to see him, to be reassured that he truly was all right.

Fortunately, she had only just finished dressing when he knocked at the door. Hurrying to answer it, she smiled at the fact that he had insisted on coming by to get her even though the rain had long since stopped and she could easily enough have walked up by herself. His complete acceptance of her as an equal in no way detracted from his instinctive gallantry. She found the combination as enjoyable as it was rare.

Logan had also taken the opportunity to shower and change into a light blue turtleneck, black slacks, and a gray blazer that emphasized the rugged grace of his body. The teasing bow he executed made her giggle, but the sound faded when she saw what he held in his hand.

Offering her the beautiful wild lily, Logan said softly, "I thought you might like this."

The smile she beamed him confirmed that she did. With the flower tucked into her hair and her hand on his arm, they strolled up the path to his house. Once inside, Jenny's eyes opened wide in surprise. Logan had clearly been busy. A table near the fireplace was set with fine linen and crystal as well as fresh flowers. The lights were turned down low. Music was playing softly from the stereo. Delicious aromas wafted from the kitchen and a bottle of wine sat waiting on the counter.

"If I didn't know better," she kidded him gently, "I'd think you were trying to seduce me."

"What makes you think you know better?"

"Why because I've already . . ." Flustered, she broke off. Logan was grinning at her so blatantly that little shivers ran up and down her spine.

He moved closer to her, so that they were almost but not quite touching. She could feel the warmth of his skin and smell the spicy sandalwood aftershave he habitually wore. "Because," he finished helpfully, "you've already been seduced?"

"Yes," Jenny admitted hesitantly. "I guess that's what I meant."

"But you're quite wrong," he murmured, closing the small distance between them to brush a tantalizing kiss against her lips. "I'm the one who's been seduced. I can't get you out of my mind, not to mention my dreams. You keep cropping up in the most unlikely places. On the mountain this morning, for instance. Even though I knew I had to concentrate, it was all I could do not to think about you."

"That's terrible! It was dangerous enough without your being distracted. You could have been hurt."

"No, I was never more sure in my life that I wouldn't be."

"I don't understand. How could you know?"

"Because," Logan explained gently, "I've never had so much to live for." The words were sealed by a long, ardent kiss that left Jenny all but breathless. When they at last drew apart, Logan's eyes glittered like quicksilver and his powerful chest rose and fell rapidly.

"I think," he muttered, "we'd better sit down to dinner

116

before we forget all about the excellent meal Maggie has undoubtedly prepared."

Dinner was superb, but Jenny remembered very little of it. She was conscious only of Logan seated across from her. Every motion he made, every word and expression, registered indelibly on her mind.

When they finished at last and rose to clear off the table, she almost sighed in relief. The effort of sitting so close to him without touching had almost been too much. She was far happier when they were settled together on the couch in front of the fireplace, his arm around her and her head nestled on his shoulder.

For a long time neither felt any need to speak. It was enough simply to share such a special, private moment. The rest of the world might not have existed, for all the thought they gave it. There was only the quiet, peaceful room, the fire, and each other.

Until Logan murmured, "Jenny, am I right to think that you've been happy here . . . in the mountains . . . with me?"

Startled, she looked up at him. "Isn't that obvious?"

He smiled faintly. "I thought it was, but I wanted to be sure. Do you miss Seattle at all?"

Did she? She liked the home she had made for herself there and was proud of it. But the plain fact was that since becoming so involved with Logan, she hadn't given a moment's thought to her life before meeting him. Nor, for that matter, had she confronted the question of the future. Stiffening slightly, she realized that must be what he was leading up to.

"No," she admitted cautiously, "I don't miss it. Why do you ask?"

"Because I was wondering if you could be happy living . . . somewhere else."

"I have lived other places," Jenny hedged, "and I've

117

enjoyed them well enough. Is that what you wanted to know, or did you have something more . . . specific in mind?"

Logan didn't respond right away. Instead, he moved just enough to let him look at her directly. Running a finger down along her cheek, he touched her mouth lightly. Her lips were moist and slightly parted. Her eyes glowed with desire she could not begin to hide. Desire and something more.

A low sigh escaped him. "Jenny, I'd like you to come and live here with me. If you can't manage it full time because of your work, then I thought we could spend part of the year in Seattle and the rest here. Either way, I don't want us to be apart."

In the first moment after his words registered, she felt no surprise. What Logan was suggesting made perfect sense in light of their obvious attachment to each other. Relief that he felt the same way as she did almost blotted out her concern that they might be jumping into something too soon. Almost but not quite.

"I don't want to be away from you either," she whispered. "But I'm just not sure I can agree to live with you. It's not something I ever envisioned for myself." Anxiously, she asked, "Is that really what you want?"

"No," Logan declared firmly, "that isn't what I want at all. I guess I didn't explain myself very well." A soft laugh escaped him. "But, then, since I've never done this before, maybe I should have expected to be a little unclear." The quicksilver eyes fastened on her held a depth of tenderness she had never seen before as he said, "Jenny, what I want is for you to marry me."

"*M-marry . . . ?*"

"Yes, you know, husband and wife, a couple. That sort of thing." Gently, he said, "I understand people do it all the time."

"But we've only known each other a few weeks. . . ."

"That's true, but some people who know each other years before they get married end up divorced. Long acquaintance isn't any guarantee of marital success. Anyway, I'd say that what we've learned about each other so far suggests very strongly that our marriage would work."

"Yes, but—" She broke off, asking herself just what she was objecting to. Logan hadn't said anything she disagreed with. On the contrary, everything he said affirmed her most deeply held hopes for them. Hopes that until that moment she had been unwilling to admit even within the privacy of her own mind.

The feelings she had experienced while waiting for him to come down Devil's Summit, and before when she had seen him fall during the earlier climb, returned in full force. For the first time in her life she had felt not simply deep concern but actual heart-wrenching fear for another's safety. In the back of her mind she had sensed the potential for that fear even before it occurred. Fundamental self-protection had forced her to try to elude it by pretending she didn't know she was head over heels in love with Logan.

Love. Such a deceptively simple word. Yet powerful enough to send her world careening end over end as the last barriers dissolved within her and she came face to face with her own emotions.

She loved Logan. Without hesitation or qualification. He was the one man she wanted to share her life with. The man who made all the little problems and compromises they would have to face inconsequential. He filled her with glorious happiness, even as he made her feel acutely vulnerable.

Swallowing hard, she murmured, "Logan, do you love me?"

He looked at her in surprise. "Didn't I say that?"

Gently, she shook her head. "No, but I'll say it first if you prefer." Taking a deep breath, she faced him bravely. "I love you and I want very much to be your wife."

"Jenny . . ." His voice caught and for just an instant there was a hint of dampness in his silvery eyes. "God, yes, I love you. More than I ever suspected it was possible to love anyone. You fill me with such joy."

It got very quiet on the couch in front of the fireplace. There was no need for words as they expressed their love in a far more fundamental way and in so doing offered each other a pledge as sacred as any vow.

When they at last moved far enough apart to gaze at each other, Logan's hair was tousled and his face flushed. He laughed shakily. "You make me forget everything. Even this."

Reaching into a pocket, he withdrew a small velvet box. "It's been in my family a long time," he explained as he gave it to Jenny. "If you don't like it, we'll get something else, but I thought you should at least see it."

He broke off as he saw the look on Jenny's face. She was staring at the ring in rapt delight. The large, perfectly formed sapphire nestled in a delicate gold filigree setting was the same shade as her eyes. Surrounded by diamonds, it shone brilliantly against her hand as Logan gently slipped it on.

Very shortly thereafter she was wearing the ring and nothing else. Standing in the center of the bedroom, Jenny remained quiet under his touch as he slowly removed each of her garments.

Logan's hands shook slightly as he pulled down the zipper of her dress and eased it from her. Her shoes and panty hose followed before he gently unhooked the front clip of her bra. As it fell open their eyes met. Hers glowed with the promise of love greater than any she had ever imagined. His were softer than she would have believed possible and shone with a light that looked very close to adoration.

As the scrap of lacy material was tossed on the floor with her other clothes, Logan cupped her breasts tenderly. His callused thumbs brushed carefully over the straining tips before he bent his head to suckle her ardently.

Jenny's fingers tangled in the silken mass of his hair, pressing him even closer. Her breath was coming in little gasps and her skin was flushed. Shimmering flames were spreading throughout her body, ignited by a blazing core of fire at the center of her being.

Quickly removing the tiny panties that were her last garment, Logan gently squeezed her buttocks as he lifted her even tighter against him. His intense arousal made her moan softly. She could not bear to be separated from him by even the slightest barrier.

Lifting her hands to the buttons of his shirt, she whispered, "Let me . . ."

It required all Logan's self-control to keep from urging her back on the bed at once. A fine sheen of perspiration glowed on his burnished chest as she slowly, lovingly, subjected him to the same delights he had given her. Only once did she hesitate, when her hands touched the zipper of his slacks. The gentle smile he gave her banished the last of her shyness.

When they stood naked together in the center of the room, Logan moved against her slowly, barely touching her as he kissed the smooth curve of her shoulders, the scented cleft between her breasts, and the taut aureoles of her nipples. Whispering words of love and desire that were alternately tender and shocking, he slid to his knees before her. Big hands held her firmly in place as his lips and tongue caressed the flat smoothness of her belly before drifting down to discover the secrets of her womanhood.

121

Engulfed in spiraling waves of pleasure, Jenny could not have stood upright by herself. Only Logan's strength kept her from collapsing. By the time he at last lifted her onto the bed, she was trembling with need.

Even so, she did not attempt to hasten their union. Instead, she gave in to the urge to learn his body as well as he knew hers. Logan's powerful fists were clenched at his sides as he struggled to control his rampaging desire long enough to fully savor her loving skill.

Poised above him, her full, swollen breasts brushing his chest, she stroked feather-light caresses along the proud arc of his brow, his strong nose, and chiseled lips. As she followed the line of his throat down to circle the flat male nipples, he trembled violently. When her mouth traced the same path, a groan tore from him.

Heady with the sense of her own feminine power, Jenny continued her enthralling exploration. She discovered that the touch of her breath alone on the smooth skin of his abdomen was enough to send tremors rippling through him. His taut thighs were similarly sensitive to her caress, as was the indentation of his navel, where her tongue lingered enticingly.

Freed of all restraint by his loving encouragement, she savored the full, driving power of his manhood until at last Logan could endure no more. Moving swiftly, he joined her in explosive fulfillment that left both utterly drained.

They slipped into sleep even as the sun began to rise above the eastern foothills into a sky swept clear of clouds and bright with the promise of a new day. As they slumbered in each other's arms, they had no hint of the painful time lying just ahead.

CHAPTER NINE

"*You're what!*" Kirsten exclaimed over the long-distance line. "*Married?* You can't get married! You've got a deadline!"

"I know, I know," Jenny laughed. "It's okay. I'll finish the article first."

"My God, you're actually serious! This isn't some weird West Coast joke?"

"No joke. I'm really going to do it. But don't you want to know to whom?"

"Oh, I already know that," Kirsten announced breezily. "Logan Kent, of course."

"How did you . . . ? I mean, I only mentioned him to you *once.*"

"It was what you didn't say. You usually talk about the people you meet on assignment. But when it came to him, you really clammed up. I knew right away something special was going on."

"You couldn't have," Jenny insisted, convinced she would never be so transparent.

"Did so. I even told Charlie we'd probably be invited to a wedding soon. There is going to be an actual wedding, isn't there? You're not going to just sneak off?"

"No, of course not. That is, there will be once we decide where it should be held. Logan's family is in Boston, mine

123

is in Philadelphia, and we both seem to have friends all over the place."

"Take my advice," her editor suggested sagely. "Don't budge from where you are right now. Get hitched out there in God's country and worry about meeting everybody later. If you go to your hometown or his, you'll be deluged by well-meaning relatives who will all think you should wait longer before taking such a monumental step that's only going to affect the entire rest of your lives forever."

"I don't suppose," Jenny muttered, "that's your subtle way of telling me you think I'm rushing into this?"

"No, it isn't," Kirsten said flatly. "I wouldn't be so presumptuous. Besides, you're a grown woman who certainly gives every evidence of knowing her own mind. I'm only speaking from personal experience."

"You mean . . ."

A long, dolorous sigh reached all the way from New York. "Charlie has *so many* relatives."

"And you've been meeting them? That sounds serious."

"It was until I met the latest batch. By the time I heard for the hundredth time what an incredible catch he is and how *astonishing* it is that I should be so lucky, I'd had enough. We aren't seeing each other for a while."

"But Kirsten, if you went so far as to start meeting his family, there must be something important between you."

"We'll see. If there is, it will all work out. If there isn't, better to find out now. Anyway, it's a good thing I'm back to concentrating on my job full time since one of my star reporters has gone all gooey-eyed and decided to splice the knot." She moaned tragically. "You probably won't write a word for weeks."

"I doubt it," Jenny assured her good-humoredly. "I've never been able to stay away from work more than a few days. Remember the last time I went on vacation? I ended up doing an article about it."

"I remember. What does Mr. Wonderful think of all that? Has he said anything about your chosen profession?"

"Only that he understands I need to keep my apartment in the city and be there some of the time. We'll alternate between his place and mine."

"Are you sure he'll go for that? There aren't any mountains to climb in Seattle."

"That's all right," Jenny said blithely. "Logan does lots more besides climb mountains."

"Oh . . . ?"

Even from three-thousand miles away, the droll tone made her blush. "I meant," she explained swiftly, "he has lots of business interests."

"That's good. They'll keep him out of mischief while you're busy. Seriously, are you sure you're going to like living out there in the backwoods?"

"Oh, I know it will be a big adjustment. But I'm certain we can work it out. It's not as though we'll be here all year round. And it is spectacularly beautiful. You should see it, Kirsten. Then you'd know what I mean."

"Is there a Bloomingdale's out there?"

"In the woods? No."

"Can you get a cab?"

"To go where? The next tree?"

"How about a Zabar's? I'd settle for even a reasonable facsimile."

"Are you still buying *all* your groceries there?" Jenny asked, remembering the superbly stocked, extravagantly priced gourmet delicatessen Kirsten had introduced her to on a trip to New York.

"Of course not. Only most of them. Answer the question."

"No, there isn't. You would undoubtedly starve, not to

125

mention having to wear twigs and branches, and walk everywhere."

"That's what I thought. I'll pass. But if you ever manage to drag God's gift to women into the caverns of Manhattan, don't you dare not give me a call first."

Jenny hung up a short time later after promising she would be in touch again soon. Talking with Kirsten always made her feel good. She was laughing softly as she walked back outside.

"Now that," a deep voice said, "is how a bride-to-be is supposed to look." Deke came toward her smiling, his green eyes gently teasing. "I can never remember if you tell the bride congratulations or best wishes, so I'll say both. And I'll throw in the wish that you always look as happy as you do right now."

"Thank you," Jenny said warmly. It meant a lot to her that Deke and the other instructors so obviously approved of the romance in their midst. She knew they had a great deal of affection and respect for Logan. The fact that they apparently thought her worthy of him touched her deeply.

"Have you set the date?"

"No, not yet, but it will probably be in a month or so. I have to go back to Seattle for a bit to complete a couple of assignments, and Logan has a few things to finish up—"

She broke off, aware that Deke was gazing at her curiously. The look was gone almost the moment it appeared, but Jenny had seen enough to be puzzled. "Is something wrong?" she asked gently.

"Uh . . . no . . . That is, what could be wrong? Everything's fine. I'm really glad for you both. You're terrific people and you deserve the best. It's just that . . . you haven't known each other very long, have you?"

"Obviously not," she said a bit tartly. Was everyone going to point that out?

Astutely, he observed, "You're already tired of hearing

that, aren't you? Okay, I'll skip that point. Just let me say that Logan is an . . . unusual man. He's my friend as well as my boss, and I don't guess there's much I wouldn't do for him. But I also wouldn't want to ever cross him, or try to push him in a direction he didn't want to go."

Jenny's back stiffened. She chose her words carefully, but her bewilderment was still clear. "Deke, you aren't seriously suggesting that I'm pushing Logan into marrying me?"

"No! Of course not. That isn't what I meant at all."

"Then what did you mean?"

"Just what I said. He's the kind of guy who knows his own mind. Any woman who married him thinking he could be changed would be in for a big letdown."

"But I don't want to change Logan. On the contrary, I love him just the way he is."

"Oh, well, that's fine then. There's no problem." His obvious relief might have been humorous if Jenny still hadn't been so puzzled about what he was talking about. But try though she did, it was clear Deke would say nothing more. A few minutes later he excused himself to get ready for class, and left her more baffled than ever.

Maggie, at least, seemed to harbor no such mysteries. She greeted Jenny with a warm hug and the assertion that she had seen it all coming. "I knew from the first time I saw you two together that you were meant for each other. It was just a question of how long it would take you both to find out." She sniffed faintly. "Must say, you sure didn't waste any time, did you?"

"I realize we haven't been acquainted very long," Jenny began in an effort to forestall the well-meaning advice she was sure was coming. But Maggie surprised her.

The housekeeper merely shrugged and said, "That doesn't matter. Why, my husband and I met only three days before we got hitched, and everything worked out

127

fine for us. Marriage is a risk any way you look at it. Knowing someone a long time, even living with him, doesn't mean you still won't be in for big surprises once you're actually Mr. and Mrs."

Unable to hide her gratitude for such magnanimity, Jenny smiled. "I guess Logan and I are used to taking risks, so we should be able to handle whatever comes at us."

"Of course you can. You seem to have all your wits about you and heaven knows he's as strong a man as you'll find anywhere. Strong and sensible." Her eyes softened as she said, "When my husband died, I thought the world had pretty much ended. Months went by with me not much good for anything. Finally, Logan came to see me. Offered me the job here. At first I didn't even want to think about it. But he made me realize I could mourn my husband and respect his memory without destroying myself. The Lord only knows where I'd be today if it hadn't been for him. And I'm not the only one. You take a close look at the backgrounds of some of the instructors here and you'll find more than one man who's needed a second chance. None of them have ever let him down either. Seems like knowing Logan trusts you is enough to pull people through even the toughest spots."

Surprised by what she had just learned about the man she was going to marry, Jenny said hesitantly, "Deke was telling me how he counted Logan as a friend and would do anything for him."

"He's only one of many," Maggie said. She smiled slightly as she added, "Don't be put out if you find yourself getting a pretty thorough look-see from people around here. Once word gets out that Logan's planning to get hitched, they'll be plenty wanting to make sure he's doing the right thing."

The thought of such widespread scrutiny made Jenny wince. Softly, she asked, "Do you think he is?"

Maggie grinned reassuringly. "Honey, no one can say that for sure, but it looks to me as though you two have a pretty good start on something special. So you just relax and enjoy yourself."

Jenny tried her best to do exactly that over the next few days as the climbing classes wound down and the rest of the students prepared to leave. Her original schedule had called for her to return to Seattle at this point, but Logan managed with very little difficulty to persuade her to stay an extra week.

"Let's get off by ourselves for a while and just relax," he suggested. "I've got a little cabin back in the woods near a not-bad trout stream. You can soak up some more local color while I work on my casting. How about it?"

"Sounds good. But is that *all* we're going to do?"

"Nooo . . ." Logan drawled teasingly. "I imagine we'll be able to come up with one or two other ways of passing the time."

Jenny giggled, sitting up in the big bed. It didn't occur to her that she no longer felt compelled to pull the sheet up to hide her breasts or indulge in any other such displays of modesty. But Logan had noted the change and appreciated it.

There was a sensual gleam in his eye as he took in the glowing length of her body that he had possessed only a short time before. It never failed to amaze him that one woman could so effortlessly stir him. Heart, mind, and body, he was enthralled by her.

Being in love was a completely new experience, one which he had frankly conflicting feelings about. On the one hand, he was delighted to discover that he had the capacity for such love and that Jenny returned it. But on the other, she made him feel acutely vulnerable in ways he did not like. The only consolation was that, so far, she didn't seem to guess how much power she had over him.

Rolling over, he trapped her under him and began tracing kisses down the line of her jaw, along her slender throat, into the scented hollow between her breasts.

"Logan . . ."

"Mmmm?"

"I . . . thought we were going to . . . fix dinner."

He looked up for just a moment. "We are. Later."

Much later. After passion had once more gentled to warm contentment, they stood side by side in the kitchen. Jenny mixed a salad while Logan prepared steaks for the broiler. She had a little difficulty chopping a sweet red pepper, which prompted him to ask, "Do you do much cooking for yourself?"

"No, I guess not. I always seem to be too busy." A smile curved her ripe mouth. "However, there is one recipe I'm very good at."

"What's that?"

"Dialing. Whenever I get really hungry, I call out for food."

"You mean pizza, hamburgers, that kind of stuff?"

"Yes."

He made a face, his distaste clear. "You can't live on that."

"I've done fine so far."

"Which is no reason to push your luck." Firmly, he said, "From now on you're going to eat sensibly, even if I have to stand over you and watch every forkful go down."

"This from the man who keeps Sara Lee brownies in his refrigerator?"

He grinned disarmingly. "Okay, I admit to one or two weaknesses. But that doesn't change my basic point. No more subsisting on junk food."

Jenny shook her head in mock distress. "No more Cheez Doodles or Sno balls?"

"You don't eat those too?" Logan demanded, looking genuinely appalled. "No one over the age of eight can eat those."

"No," she admitted. "But I have snuggled up with a pint of really good ice cream from time to time."

"Oh, well, that's all right . . ."

"Hardly. It goes straight to my hips."

A heartwarming leer lit his quicksilver eyes. "I'm very partial to your hips."

"I'd noticed," Jenny murmured contentedly.

"Also your—"

Seeing the conversation getting rapidly out of hand, she interrupted firmly. "I get the message. Now, about dinner . . ."

Reluctantly, he turned back to the steaks. They enjoyed a leisurely meal in front of the fireplace, then went to bed early, planning to leave for the fishing cabin first thing the next morning.

Although she was looking forward to spending a week alone with Logan, Jenny had trouble responding when he woke her just before dawn. Still pleasantly satiated from a night that had turned out to be rather more vigorous than originally intended, she wanted to sleep for several more hours.

Burrowing her head into the pillows, she muttered, "Go 'way."

"Not a chance," Logan laughed. She had already noticed that he had a habit of being distressingly cheerful early in the morning. Now he seemed determined to outdo himself. Pushing open the curtains, he announced, "It's a beautiful day. You should be raring to go."

A moan of protest broke from her at the sudden intrusion of light. "I am," she croaked. "Back to sleep."

131

"I made coffee," Logan cajoled.

"Goody. Keep mine warm for me."

"And cinnamon rolls."

"Not hungry."

He was silent for a moment before sighing resignedly. "This obviously calls for sterner measures." A lean hand darted out, ripping the covers from her and exposing her naked body to the cool morning air.

"*Argh!*"

"There, there," Logan soothed her as he scooped her limp form off the bed. "It's not so bad. You'll feel better in a few minutes."

"I hate you."

"Are you always this cheerful in the morning?"

"No, I'm usually worse. We may have to have separate rooms."

"I don't think so," Logan said firmly, depositing her in the bathroom. He reached in and turned on the shower. "I'll be back in five minutes. If you're not out by then, I'll figure you've fallen asleep and come in after you."

"*Sadist!*" Muttering to herself, Jenny slipped cautiously under the water. She wouldn't put it past him to have turned on only the cold. But instead the shower was pleasantly warm yet invigorating.

Moments later she was fully awake and willing to admit that she was glad of it. Not that she would tell Logan that. There was such a thing as being too agreeable, even with the man she loved.

The reminder of how she felt about him cheered her up. She smiled as she soaped and rinsed her body, then shampooed her hair. Wondering how much of the allotted five minutes were left, she stepped out of the shower straight into a big, soft towel.

Logan grinned down at her as he began to gently dry her hair. "Do you always sing in the shower?"

132

"I wasn't," Jenny protested, struggling to ignore the effect his touch was having on her.

"You were humming."

"Really? I didn't know I did that."

"Stick with me, kid. You'll find out all sorts of great stuff."

"I already have," she informed him archly. "For instance, did you know you have dimples on you bottom?"

"*I what?*"

"Dimples, real cute ones. Don't tell me no one ever mentioned them before?"

"Somehow," Logan muttered, "the subject never came up."

Jenny wasn't surprised. She suspected his past relationships hadn't been the sort that encouraged such observances. Nonetheless, the thought of him with other women rankled.

He caught her scowl and laughed softly. "Looks as though there's something else you need to learn."

"What's that?" Jenny asked doubtfully.

"How special you are to me. You're completely apart from everything I've experienced in the past and you've totally changed my view of the future."

Soothed, she smiled at him provocatively. "When we get to this cabin you're so fond of, do you suppose we could continue my lessons?"

"Well, I don't know. . . . I am pretty anxious to do some fishing."

"*Why you . . . !*"

Laughing, he dodged the small fists aimed at his chest. "I might be persuaded, but only if you get dressed and downstairs in record time."

"Just for that, I'm tempted to stay up here."

"Oh?" His hand moving down her back and around to lightly brush her breasts convinced her such stubbornness

133

would serve no purpose. Half an hour later she had dressed, breakfasted, and helped load their luggage and supplies into the jeep.

Hefting her suitcase, Logan groaned. "What on earth is in here? Part of a mountain?"

"Just my clothes and equipment."

"You mean your camera?"

"That and my extra lenses, film, notebooks, dictaphone . . ."

"Hold on! Do you always travel with this much stuff?"

"It's not a lot," Jenny insisted. "Plenty of photojournalists I know pack far more stuff."

"But you're going off for a week in the woods, not a month on assignment at the ends of the earth."

"You said yourself I'd be able to pick up local color while you fish. So I have to be able to take photos and notes."

"God help me," Logan grumbled as he hoisted the case into the back of the jeep. "If this is what you take for a few days of fishing, who knows what you'll feel you can't live without on our honeymoon."

"I didn't realize we were going on one," Jenny pointed out as she settled into the seat next to him. "Did you have any place in particular in mind?"

"Yes. Someplace with absolutely no newsworthy features and one very large bed."

"Don't you think you can keep me sufficiently distracted if we go someplace interesting?"

"I think," Logan muttered, "you'd better watch yourself or I'm going to pull over to the side of the road and give the squirrels something to really chatter about."

Not absolutely certain that he was kidding, Jenny fell wisely silent. She gave herself up to pleasant thoughts about where they might honeymoon as Logan maneuvered the jeep along increasingly rough, narrow roads until at last they veered onto a path that was so bumpy she had to abandon her daydreams in favor of keeping her balance.

"Who discovered this great fishing spot?" she muttered, holding on to the side and trying not to bounce up and down too much. "A cow? That's certainly what blazed this trail."

"Be glad there's any road at all," Logan suggested good-naturedly. "Otherwise we'd have to backpack it. And with all that stuff you insisted on bringing, I'd hate to think what kind of shape you'd be in by the time you finally made it."

"Do you mean to tell me," Jenny demanded in mock outrage, "you'd expect me to carry my own bag?"

"Sure would. Isn't that what liberation is all about?"

A very unladylike snort broke from her. "You know perfectly well it isn't."

"How can you be so sure of what I think?" Logan hedged.

"Because," Jenny explained tolerantly, "you're too smart to take such a simplistic view of something so complicated. I know perfectly well you consider me an equal, but that doesn't mean we have to be able to do all the same things. It seems to me that men and women can fall in love and build lives together precisely because we are different. We have complementary skills and perceptions that we can use to help each other."

Agreement mixed with just a touch of chagrin as Logan looked at Jenny. "Sounds as though I don't have a chance of coming off real macho with you."

Jenny laughed softly. "Why would you want to? The macho types I've met, I wouldn't get close to with a big stick. While with you . . ."

"Yesss . . ."

Her indigo eyes darkened teasingly. "If you can tear yourself away from the fishing long enough, I'll be happy to show you exactly why being sensitive and caring beats being macho any day."

"You've got a deal," Logan informed her succinctly. "Who needs a whole lot of dead fish, anyway?"

"We do," Jenny insisted, "at least, if those supplies in the back are anything to go by. Do you really expect to live on them for a whole week?"

"Aren't you the one who was bemoaning the state of her hips?"

"Not exactly."

"Anyway, don't worry about it. I keep the cabin storeroom well stocked."

A few minutes later she saw what he meant.

The cabin nestled in a grove of pine trees was small and rustic, but nonetheless comfortable. The single room was dominated by a large stone fireplace and simply furnished with a bed, table, bookshelves, and racks for hunting and fishing equipment. Brightly colored woven rugs and a quilted bedspread made it warm and cheery.

The tiny kitchen was hardly luxurious, but it still had everything required for producing ample meals. Next to it, the storeroom Logan had mentioned was full of canned and dried goods, all carefully sealed and organized to make it easy to find anything in a hurry.

There was even an indoor bath, which Jenny claimed destroyed her illusions of the rugged living she had presumed he enjoyed in the backwoods.

"Have you ever," Logan asked dryly, "made your way to an outhouse late at night in the dead of winter?"

"As a matter of fact, I have. In fact, it would be an exaggeration to call what I was heading for an outhouse."

"Then you know why I drew the line at doing without indoor plumbing. I'm all for roughing it, but there are limits."

Jenny agreed completely. She thought the cabin was a

perfect blend of simplicity and comfort. While Logan unloaded the jeep, she made coffee and sandwiches, which they ate while sitting on the small porch that fronted on the river. Afterward, they walked down to the water so that Logan could point out the best fishing spots.

"Have you been coming here long?" Jenny asked after he had regaled her with several stories about massive trout and salmon pulled from the sparkling depths.

"Since I first discovered the Cascades. One of the guys I climbed with owned this place then. But he didn't get to use it much, so I bought it. I lived out here all of one year, staying on through the winter even though that wasn't supposed to be a good idea." He smiled slightly. "Worked fine for me. I had a chance to do some thinking and make some pretty basic decisions about my life."

"Is that when you decided to start the school?" Jenny asked, sitting down near a cluster of violets blooming in the shade of a pine tree.

Logan joined her there. "Yes. I wanted a base of operations for my other business interests, and this seemed as good a place as any."

"You didn't feel drawn to a big city at all?"

"Can't say I did. I've lived in half a dozen of them, and while they all had something special to offer, it never quite seemed to outweigh the negative aspects." Perceptively, he added, "But don't let that worry you. I know we'll need to live in Seattle part of the time and I'm sure I'll adjust to it."

Leaning back against the tree, he looked at her closely as he said, "What I'm not so sure about is how you're going to feel living out here. Have you thought anymore about that?"

"Yes," Jenny admitted, relaxing in the circle of his arm. "But I don't see why it should be a problem. I like it here."

"You like it after a few weeks. But how will you feel

after several months?" Worriedly, he said, "You may get bored."

Glancing up at him through the thick fringe of her lashes, she gave in to the temptation to tease him and murmured, "I'd say it's your job to make sure that doesn't happen."

Logan laughed, rightly judging that if she was not particularly concerned, there was no reason for him to be. But falling in with her playfulness, he said, "Then I'd better start now. How about a swim?"

Jenny looked down at the fast-rushing river a bit dubiously. "In there?"

"Only if you're part salmon. No, there's a rock pool a short distance behind the cabin. It's calm as a bathtub and with the bright sun we've had all day, probably about as warm."

"Sounds great." Getting up quickly she started off down the path without waiting for him. When she had gone several feet, she glanced back over her shoulder. "Just one thing though. I hope you won't mind that I didn't bring a suit."

Logan's deep laugh startled a blue jay. It cawed at them shrilly as they walked hand in hand toward the pool.

The pure blue tarn folded between glacier-strewn boulders was everything Logan had promised, and then some. Surrounded by fragrant manzanita and laurel bushes, it was as tranquil and beckoning as a tropical lagoon. More so, Jenny thought, because she had never had the opportunity to share a lagoon with Logan, whereas now . . .

"Last one in cooks supper," he announced suddenly, stripping off his shirt.

Jenny wasted no time following suit. Within minutes they were both buck naked and diving into the water. It was a toss-up who made it in first, though Logan claimed the victory.

"You wear more clothes than I do," he insisted, "so you couldn't have beat me in."

"Oh, all right," Jenny relented in mock resignation. "I'll cook dinner." She treaded water as she pretended to consider the menu. "Let me see now . . . do we have any corn flakes? Or maybe Pop-tarts would be better. Got any of those?"

"Never mind," Logan groaned. "I'll fix dinner. But don't expect to get away with this once we're married. One of my wedding gifts to you is definitely going to be a cookbook."

Floating on her back, she regarded him appreciatively. Standing upright as he still was, with the water coming only as high as his narrow hips, he looked supremely male. Sunlight bouncing off the wide sweep of his shoulders and chest emphasized the bronze hue of his skin. Golden hairs, almost as light as the ashen curls clinging to his well-shaped head, glistened. Clearly defined muscles rippled as he lowered himself into the water and swam toward her.

A shiver of anticipation ran along her spine. Glancing down the length of her body, pale under the shimmering water, she saw that her nipples were hard. Logan noticed them, too, and laughed softly.

"Come over here."

His commanding tone ignited a mutinous spark deep within her. Feigning innocence of what he had in mind, she countered, "Why should I?"

"Because you want to."

That was hard to argue with, but Jenny was determined not to let him have everything his own way. She swam closer, but stopped just beyond his grasp. Logan frowned. "Has anyone ever told you you're very stubborn?"

"Surely you mentioned that somewhere along the line."

"Well, just in case I haven't—" He broke off suddenly and without any warning dove under the water, closing the small remaining distance between them in a single stroke.

Jenny yelped as he seized her around the hips, pulling her under with him. She had just enough time to take a deep breath before the water closed over her head.

Her dark-umber hair swirled around them both as their bodies touched, limbs entwining. Logan's mouth was cool and wet against her own, his tongue instantly demanding entrance. The shock of his passionate kiss quaked through her, evoking a silent moan of acceptance and surrender. Without hesitation her arms closed around him. Swept by undulating waves of pleasure, she pressed as close as she could get to his potent length.

Their feet brushed against the bottom of the pond for just an instant before Logan swiftly kicked them back to the surface. As they broke water, both were panting for air, but neither had any intention of stopping.

Still touching, they swam toward the shore. As they reached it, Logan stood up and lifted Jenny high against his chest. He strode out of the water, laying her on the ground near their clothes.

Lowering himself beside her, he murmured, "Are you comfortable? The ground doesn't hurt your back?"

A wicked grin curved her mouth. "Now that you mention it, it is awful scratchy."

Logan was about to resign himself to waiting however long it took them to get back to the cabin, when she surprised him. Sitting up, her small but strong hands pushed against his shoulders.

"Let's change places."

He was only too happy to agree. Stretched out beneath her, he gave himself up to her ardent care.

For Jenny, the next few minutes were a revelation in her own capacity for passion as well as his response. She allowed herself the luxury of touching him slowly, searching out all his most sensitive spots and exploring them to the fullest.

Her lips brushed tenderly over his nipples, delighting in the way they hardened in her mouth. Moving downward along the hard, sinewy line of his chest, she followed the mat of golden hair that tapered beneath his waist before thickening again at his groin.

Licking all around his navel, she smiled at his gasp, making the sound repeat even more urgently when she at last gave in to the need to know him as intimately as he knew her.

Slowly, persistently, she brought him again and again to the edge of rapture until his powerful body was shaken by repeating tremors and she knew he could bear very little more.

Only then did she at last give in to her own fierce hunger and draw him within her.

Long moments later they lay replete in each other's arms. Logan brushed a tender hand over her hair and laughed gently. "Something tells me you'll still be astonishing me when we're both old and gray and sitting in our rockers out on the front porch."

"Rockers, hmmm . . . I wonder?" she giggled impishly. "No, I suppose not. We wouldn't want to shock the neighbors."

"That does it, woman!" Standing quickly, Logan scooped her up. Jenny had barely a moment to grab their clothes before he was striding toward the cabin with her nestled in his arms.

Wrapped in a warm robe, she settled in front of the huge stone fireplace to dry her hair while Logan started dinner. They ate early, both tired out from the events of the last few days. Darkness had barely settled fully over the fragrant pine trees and soft green firs before they banked the fire and crawled into bed.

Lying close against him, Jenny relished the sense of utter contentment that swept over her. She had no doubt she was exactly where she belonged and where she wanted to be for the rest of her life. The thought that she would soon be his wife filled her with joy. Softly, she murmured, "Have you given any more thought to setting a date?"

Logan was almost asleep but he answered nonetheless. "Hmmm. I'd like it to be soon."

"Let's see, we have to find a place to have it, notify our family and friends, pick a honeymoon spot. Then there's the dress . . . Would next month be all right?"

"Can't."

Jenny opened her eyes. "Why not?"

"Because," he murmured drowsily, "next month I'll be climbing Mount McKinley again."

And having dropped that stunning piece of news on her, he turned over and fell promptly asleep.

CHAPTER TEN

"I just don't understand how you can take this attitude," Jenny protested tightly. "Doesn't it mean anything to you that you've said you love me and want us to have a life together?"

From his position near the fireplace, Logan scowled at her. They had been arguing since shortly after he woke an hour before. He had tried to understand her point of view, but so far had failed utterly. The result left him frustrated and angry.

"Of course it does," he snapped. "But I might ask you the same question. What on earth made you think that because we're going to be married I'd give up climbing?"

Seated in the center of the bed, dressed in jeans and a sweater that she had pulled on before dawn when she finally gave up the futile struggle to sleep, Jenny shook her head wearily. "I never thought that. But running the school and making rescue climbs aren't the same as deliberately risking your life on an ascent that has already killed seven of your friends and may just as well kill you the next time around."

A dark flush stained Logan's cheeks. "Thanks for the vote of confidence."

She shook her head impatiently. "It has nothing to do with my respect for you as a climber. I know you're one of the best. But that didn't matter the last time you went up Mount McKinley, did it? Your friends still died and you came pretty close to joining them. Or did you think I didn't know much about that?"

"I had no idea what you knew about it," he insisted. "It never occurred to me to wonder."

"You mean you never considered that I might be upset by these plans?"

"No, it didn't. We both know *you've* done some pretty hair-raising things in the course of *your* career. So I guess if I thought of it at all, I just figured you'd understand."

His grudging tone said plainly that he felt she was at fault for not doing so. Jenny stared at him in dismay. The man she loved, whom she thought she knew well enough to marry, seemed to have turned into a stranger before her eyes.

"You figured wrong," she murmured, no longer trying to hide her pain. "And I don't believe for a moment that you honestly think what I do in the course of my work compares with your desire to risk your life on some mountain."

"Why not?" Logan challenged her. "What's so all-fired sacred about your work that any risks are justified? The world wouldn't come to an end if your articles and photos didn't get printed."

Sliding off the bed, Jenny stalked over to him. She glared icily as she said, "I never said it would. But at least people get some benefit from what I do, whereas—"

"Hold it. Are you actually suggesting what I do is a waste of time?"

"No, not exactly. I know you and the other people involved in a climb get a tremendous amount out of it. But no one else does. It's a very . . . selfish activity."

"*Selfish?*" Logan repeated disbelievingly. "What the hell is that supposed to mean?"

"Just what it seems to. You climb for your own sake,

not anyone else's. And that's fine. If we all went around making grandiose gestures for the welfare of humanity, it would be a pretty tedious world. But you have to think of more than yourself now." Unsteadily, she added, "Or at least you should be willing to if you really love me."

"I can't believe you're saying this. You're seriously making my decision to climb Mount McKinley a test of whether or not I love you?"

"I didn't put it that way," Jenny protested weakly.

"You came damn close."

His seemingly callous intransigence snapped the thin hold she had maintained on her temper. The dread that had grown in her all night long as she lay awake envisioning him in one life-threatening situation after another abruptly spiraled out of control.

Her fists clenched at her sides as she said, "All right then! If you want to lay it out in those terms, go ahead. I don't want you to make the climb because I'm afraid you'll be killed. It's torture just to think of your going back up that mountain. If you love me, how can you subject me to that?"

Logan's hard features softened slightly as he took in the full extent of her distress. Silently, he admitted that he would have to get used to someone caring about him so deeply. It was a new experience he was handling badly.

In an effort to recover lost ground and help her understand his own view of the situation, he said gently, "There's more involved in this than just you and me. Everybody who attempted the climb last year and survived is part of this new effort. We have to do it both to honor our friends who died and to regain our own confidence. Even if we don't make it to the top, we have to know that we were able to get back on that mountain despite what happened."

His hope that she would be able to see his point of view

145

vanished as Jenny shook her head disconsolately. "So for your friends and for some twisted sense of honor, you want to risk your life? That's more important to you than how I feel?"

Turning away from her, he shoved his hands deep into his pockets and stared out the window. So softly that she had to strain to hear him he asked, "Who's being selfish now?"

"I'm not!"

In the reflection of the glass, their gazes locked. "Aren't you?" he demanded. "All I've heard so far is how I'm supposed to act if I really love you. But what about your own actions? You haven't shown the slightest willingness to understand my feelings, much less try to accept them."

"That isn't fair. It's you I'm thinking of. If you're hurt or—"

"Cut it out, Jenny! We've got enough of a problem here without your lying to yourself. If you were thinking of me, you'd be able to at least consider why I feel the climb is so important. But you're not, are you? All you're taking into account are your own feelings."

She stared at him resentfully, convinced that he was twisting everything she said to suit his own self-centered purposes. Only the fact that she cared for him so desperately made her try to explain. "You don't have any sense of your own mortality, Logan. If you did, you wouldn't be able to do the things you do. But I've seen you bruised and exhausted. I know you can be hurt, or worse."

His throat tightened as he listened to her. She was so beautiful, so beyond anything he had ever known. And she loved him. Or at least she believed she did. Struggling to come to terms with the sincerity of her fears, he said, "Jenny, for both our sakes, try to turn around what you just said. Suppose there was a story you really wanted to cover, that you thought was important for itself and for what it could contribute to your development as a journalist. And suppose I asked you not to go because it was dangerous. How would you feel?"

"I . . ." She hesitated, realizing there was no simple response. "I'm not sure because it hasn't actually happened. But I'd like to think that if I agreed with you about its being risky, I'd put your feelings first and not go."

"No matter what it meant to you personally?"

"*You* mean more, Logan. That's the whole point."

He had no answer to that. She was asking him to give up a dream he had cherished for more than a year. A dream that was an integral part of his identity as a man. Yet she claimed to love him. He couldn't reconcile the apparent contradiction.

"Jenny," he said at last, "I think we both need some time to consider this. I'm going fishing for a while. Will you be all right here?"

She nodded. She too wanted to be alone to consider the situation. However upset she might be, Logan's mere presence was enough to distract her. With him gone, perhaps she would be able to think more clearly.

But half an hour later, after he had gathered his fishing gear and headed down toward the river, she wondered if there was in fact anything left to think about. He seemed to take it for granted that she would have no say in what he chose to do. His life would go on exactly as he planned no matter how much pain it caused her. Was that the behavior of a man in love?

Doubting him, doubting herself, Jenny paced back and forth across the small room. Too clearly she remembered Deke's warning that Logan was not a man any woman could change. The young instructor had obviously known about the climb, perhaps was even planning to take part in it. So he must share Logan's depth of commitment to the venture. But he, at least, had been able to anticipate her feelings and understand them, whereas Logan seemed not to care how she felt.

Unable to tolerate the closed-in feeling of the cabin, she went outside. Except for the occasional chirps of thrushes and wrens nesting in the nearby trees, it was very quiet. Logan was nowhere in sight. She guessed he was farther down the river at one of the favorite casting spots he had shown her.

Walking on a bit farther, she settled finally on a fallen log and set herself to do some serious thinking. Her reporter's training predisposed her to try to look at any question objectively, so, difficult though it was, she made a genuine effort to understand Logan's point of view.

Since coming into manhood, he had taken full responsibility for his life and made all his own decisions without having to worry about the needs or reactions of anyone else. Though she did not doubt he loved his family, that had not stopped him from taking risks that must have caused them great concern. Yet they very wisely afforded him the respect due any independent, rational adult and did not try to impinge on how he ran his life.

So far, so good. She respected what he had done and shared his determination to live to the fullest possible extent of his potential. But beyond that, she ran straight up against the wall of her own feelings.

Although she had never experienced it before, she firmly believed that love between a man and a woman was different from any other emotion. Children, however cherished they were, grew up and went away. That was part of the natural order and had to be accepted as such. But ideally at least, a husband and wife were together forever. How could there be any hope of achieving such long-term unity unless they were both willing to make compromises and even sacrifices for the sake of the other?

Was she really asking Logan for something so difficult?

148

She didn't want him to needlessly risk the life that had become such an integral part of her own. She wanted him to remain whole and strong, to be with her as a husband, lover, and friend, and someday perhaps to be the father of her children. The thought that he might instead end up crushed under tons of snow and ice was an open wound throbbing inside her.

Yet that didn't seem to matter to him at all.

Slowly, falteringly, she was forced to the conclusion that if he loved her in the way he must for them to share a lifetime together, he would not be able to subject her to such pain.

Tears turned her eyes to luminescent pools as she considered that perhaps it would have been wiser after all if they had known each other longer before becoming so involved. Maybe then they would have achieved a better understanding of each other's feelings and needs on which to base a lifelong commitment.

But it was too late to think of that. In fact, it was too late for a great deal. Unless Logan had changed his mind about what was really most important to him.

By the time she finally made her way back, hours had passed. The confrontation with herself had left her wearier than any physical effort could ever manage. It was a struggle just to put one foot in front of the other.

Rounding the last bend before the cabin, her step faltered. A fishing rod was propped outside the door. Logan was back.

Reluctantly, she forced herself to go on. There was nothing to be gained from delay except further anguish. Taking a deep breath, she pushed open the door and walked inside.

He was standing in the center of the room, looking almost exactly as she had last seen him. His back was to her and his hands were deep inside his pockets. His powerful shoulders were slightly stooped.

Softly, not wanting to startle him, she murmured, "Did you catch anything?"

At the first sound of her voice, Logan turned. His eyes were expressionless and his mouth was drawn in a hard line. "No, but I did quite a lot of thinking."

She swallowed tightly. "So did I."

"And . . ."

"I still feel the same way, Logan. I love you and I don't want you to be hurt. That seems perfectly understandable to me. What I can't see is why my feelings apparently don't count much with you."

He shook his head impatiently. "They do count. I keep telling you that, but you don't listen."

A small, sad smile curved Jenny's mouth. "Haven't you heard that actions speak louder than words? Will you still be saying how much you love me and want us to be together when you're falling off that mountain?"

"I am not going to fall! Why do you keep insisting that the worst will happen?"

"Why do you keep refusing to consider the possibility? You aren't Superman. You're human, like the rest of us. Every bit as vulnerable and, in the final analysis, fragile. I've seen how easily people can die. Don't try to tell me it won't happen to you."

She broke off, perilously close to tears she was determined he would not see.

"I'm not trying to tell you that," he insisted. "I'd have to be an idiot not to know I can die on a mountain. But the point is, if I don't at least try to make the climb, something vital is going to die inside me. That's what you don't seem able to understand."

"No," Jenny agreed sorrowfully, "I don't. I don't see why you think we should get married if the way we feel

150

about each other isn't the most important thing in your life. If something else counts for more, this 'vital' something that's going to die in you, then you just aren't ready for the kind of commitment I need."

Logan stared at her for what seemed like a very long time before at last he nodded grimly. "Maybe I'm not. And maybe you aren't ready for the kind of supportive relationship I hoped we would have. It seems that our ideas about what makes a marriage are too different to be reconciled."

She opened her mouth to refute what he had just said, only to close it again without uttering a word. There really was nothing more to say. Silently, she went over to the closet and got her suitcase out.

CHAPTER ELEVEN

"I'll be fine, Kirsten," Jenny insisted. "There's no reason to be worried about me."

"You sure don't sound fine. I'll bet you don't look it either. Are you taking care of yourself?"

"Yes, of course I am. Recent evidence not to the contrary, I am capable of looking after myself."

The hint of bitterness in her voice was impossible to deny. Kirsten sighed sympathetically. "Maybe it would help to talk about it."

"I've already told you the whole story. We rushed into a relationship before we really knew each other. Logan is a wonderful man, we just aren't meant to make a life together."

"If you say so . . ."

"It's like you said when you stopped seeing Charlie. Better to find out you're incompatible before getting married rather than afterward."

There was a moment's silence before Kirsten said hesitantly, "Charlie and I are back together."

Jenny's eyes, red-rimmed from lack of sleep and several unavoidable bouts of crying, widened. For the first time in days she smiled. Despite her own sadness she was genuinely happy for her friend. "I'm so glad. I don't know anyone who deserves more of all the good things than you." A bit wistfully, she added, "You really do love him, don't you?"

"Yes, I guess I do, although sometimes I wonder why."

Puzzled, Jenny straightened up slightly in the chair in front of her word processor. She dragged her gaze from the window overlooking Puget Sound and focused more firmly on the conversation. "What do you mean?"

Kirsten laughed gently. "Oh, it's just that we seem to disagree about everything. We argue all the time about the stupidest things—which restaurant to eat at, which movie to see, the ties he wears, the books I read. You know."

No, Jenny didn't know. She and Logan hadn't been together long enough to discover such details about each other. Tentatively, she asked, "But you agree about the really big issues, don't you?"

"Well, sort of . . . He wants to have children soon, I want to wait awhile. He wants to live in the suburbs when we have a family. I envision a nice apartment near Central Park. I'm not too happy about all the traveling he has to do. He's not crazy the fact that I earn more money. But," she concluded cheerfully, "we'll work it all out."

Loyalty to her friend forced Jenny to agree. But privately she was baffled by how Kirsten could sound so calm about loving a man with whom she had such basic differences. She couldn't quite resist the urge to ask, "How can you be so sure? I mean, marriage is such a big risk anyway without adding any other problems."

A bemused chuckle darted over the phone line. "Did I hear correctly? Is this the same Jenny Hammond who wrote those articles about rafting down the Amazon and got those great photos of an ice floe breaking up near the Arctic? You're worrying about taking risks?"

"That was different. Physical danger isn't anywhere near as scary as the thought of getting really wrecked emotionally."

There was a moment's silence before Kirsten asked gently, "Is that what happened? Did you and Logan break up because you were afraid of getting hurt?"

Blinking rapidly, Jenny made a valiant effort to sound calm and composed. "It was more a case of my being worried about him getting hurt, and him not caring."

"Maybe it's the three-thousand miles or so between us, but that didn't come across too clearly. Want to try again?"

Reluctantly, trying not to burden her friend with her problems, she explained. "Logan is planning to lead another expedition up Mount McKinley to attempt the same route he tried last year, where seven climbers were killed. I tried to explain to him that I can't live with the thought that this time he'll end up on the long roster of victims that mountain has claimed. But he just wouldn't understand. His freedom to do anything he chooses is more important to him than anything else."

"Oh, now I'm beginning to understand. You're really stuck, aren't you?"

"Not really," Jenny insisted. "I had the option to leave and I took it."

"That's fine, if it works. I hope for your sake you'll be able to put the whole experience behind you. That would be the best possible indication that you were right to leave because what you felt for each other wasn't strong enough to make a marriage. But don't be too surprised if that isn't the way it turns out."

Jenny wasn't quite prepared to admit she had already begun to suspect it wouldn't, but she did ask, "Is that why you got back together with Charlie?"

"Exactly. Despite all the disagreements, the annoyances, the very real problems we have, being without him was far worse." Kirsten laughed softly. "You know, people like to think that love is bliss. Springtime and roses,

154

eternal sunshine, and one wonderful day after another. It isn't that at all. It can be sheer hell."

"You're not kidding," Jenny muttered. Since leaving Logan the week before, she had discovered the true depth of pain she was capable of experiencing. Nothing seemed to ease it. Not time, or work, or any of her increasingly desperate attempts to bar him from her thoughts and dreams.

Everything else in her life faded into insignificance when compared with the hold he had on her. But she couldn't claim to be surprised by that. She had left, knowing that she loved him. Her feelings were never the issue. It was his lack of commitment that had driven her away.

She said as much to Kirsten, who was kind enough to hear her out before responding, "There's only one way I know of to settle what you're going through. You have to ask yourself which is better—being without him or suffering the worst thing that could happen if you stayed with him. That was the toughest question for me to answer, and I think it may be the same for you. You just might discover that you have to take him on his own terms, because the alternative is intolerable."

Jenny thought about that long after she hung up. There was a good chance Kirsten was right. Did she really want to go on living in a world that contained no joy or purpose, that lacked even the anticipation of better times to come? Without Logan the simple pleasure of being alive which she had always before taken for granted was gone. She was merely going through the motions of existing.

Getting up, she wandered into the kitchen to make a cup of coffee, ignoring the fact that it was barely afternoon and she'd already had six. Outside, the day was brilliantly clear. Sun-washed streets of neat rowhouses beckoned. She could go out for a walk, perhaps wander over to the sprawling Farmers' Market and do some shopping.

The idea was rejected almost as soon as it occurred. In the last few days she had walked all over her adopted city, rediscovering neighborhoods she hadn't wandered into in years. Starting at the restored waterfront with its numerous shops and restaurants, she had visited all Seattle's high points and even gone so far as to ride the ferry back and forth to the picturesque islands lying just off its shores.

All she had gotten out of her excursions were sore feet and the knowledge that the days were ticking away to her deadline on the climbing-school article, but so far she had not managed to write a word.

In the large closet she had converted to a darkroom, prints from the numerous rows of film she had shot were drying. Jenny peered at them dispiritedly.

So what if she had taken some of the best pictures of her life? That no longer gave her much satisfaction. The scenes of the mountains were breathtaking, but she afforded them barely a glance. All her attention was held by the photos of Logan. She hadn't realized she had taken so many of him. But there he was, working with a student, scaling a rock face, talking with Deke. She saw his long, powerful form stretched out beside a riverbank as he caught a quick nap, a breeze lifting his silvery hair as he sat bare-chested mending a rope harness, his slate-gray eyes crinkling slightly as he smiled at her.

A sob caught in her throat. She fled from the darkroom, slamming the door behind her.

The strain of not eating or sleeping properly was beginning to take a serious toll. There were mauve shadows beneath her eyes. The healthy apricot glow of her skin had vanished. She was pale and almost fragile-looking. Worst of all, she was losing all confidence in herself. Her inability to work plagued her. The creativity that had always been her greatest source of pride and satisfaction seemed to have vanished. The thought that it might never return terrified her.

She simply couldn't go on like that.

Putting down the coffee cup she had carried with her from room to room, Jenny marched herself into the shower. She stripped off her clothes and stood under it full blast. Scrubbing herself vigorously, she kept her mind blank. When her hair was dry and she was dressed in clean jeans and a T-shirt, she went back out to the kitchen and fixed a salad and a bowl of soup.

In a final all-out effort at reviving herself, she pulled open all the curtains so that the apartment was flooded with sunlight, put a favorite symphony on the stereo, and determinedly plunked down in front of her word processor.

The words came with excruciating slowness, but they did at last take form. She went through her notes meticulously, forcing herself to relive moments with Logan no matter how painful they were. Several times she got up to consult the photos still in the darkroom, deciding how an idea might best be presented to correspond with the article's illustrations.

In doing so, she could not avoid seeing his image over and over. His features stared at her from the prints, his words spoke from the pages of her notebooks. The echo of his touch sounded deep within her, stirring memories of the ecstasy they had found together.

She worked far into the night, knowing that it was useless to try to sleep until she was mentally and physically exhausted. By the time she at last switched off the computer and headed for bed, it was well after midnight. The first draft of the article was done. With that knowledge to console her, she crept under the covers. For the first time in a week, consciousness slipped away the moment her eyes closed.

Bright and early the next morning she was back at work. Eating breakfast at her desk, she began the tedious but essential process of rewriting. By afternoon the article was done. Connecting her computer to the phone lines, she transmitted the copy to *WomanWorld* and went back to developing her pictures. An hour later the phone rang.

"Do I have to tell you how good it is?" Kirsten asked.

"Yes, you know I love that kind of talk."

Her friend laughed tolerantly. "To be honest, I'm very surprised. I thought you'd hardly be able to write at all, much less turn out something of this caliber."

"Maybe I just thrive on adversity."

"I don't think so, but seriously, how are you doing?"

"I—I'm not sure . . ."

She wasn't trying to be evasive. It was just that since buckling down to work the day before, she had managed to keep her relationship with Logan from dominating her thoughts as it had until then. She had certainly been thinking about him, but not with the same painful intensity as before. Now she realized that while consciously her mind had seemed to be on other things, subconsciously a great deal had been going on.

She missed him so terribly. It was as though some vital part of herself had been cut away. Realizing that, she remembered what he had said about the importance of the climb to him. Was this desolate emptiness what Logan had anticipated when she asked him to forgo the Mount McKinley expedition? If so, she could understand why he had so vehemently refused.

It still made no sense to her that he would want to risk his life in such a venture, but that didn't prevent her from perceiving why no one would willingly subject himself to such inner devastation.

"Are you still there?" Kirsten asked suddenly.

"What? Oh, yes. Sorry, I guess I sort of faded off."

"That's okay. I get the picture. Speaking of which—"

"I'll send the photos to you tomorrow, as soon as I've made my final selections."

"Are they as good as the article?"

Jenny laughed with a touch of her old self. "Better."

"This I've got to see." Kirsten paused for a moment before she asked, "If I need to get in touch with you in the next few days, where will you be?"

About to say that she would be at her apartment, Jenny hesitated. The thought of the empty days and nights that stretched out before her was acutely painful. She needed Logan more than she had ever thought it possible to need anyone but herself. Needed him enough so that emotional safety and pride offered no more than the most superficial solace. Perhaps even needed him enough to do what Kirsten had already predicted would happen, acceptance of him on his own terms.

"I may be away for a while. If I am, I'll let you know."

There was a definite note of satisfaction in her friend's voice as she said, "Fine. I probably won't have to be in touch with you at all, since the story is coming together this well, but I would like to know how you are."

Touched by what she knew to be deep concern tempered by consideration for her privacy, Jenny said, "Remember I told you yesterday that I'd be fine? Well, this time I really mean it."

Her determined tone won a chuckle from Kirsten. "That's the spirit. When you come out swinging, you can't be beat." Making it clear she knew exactly what her friend was contemplating, she added, "I almost feel sorry for Mr. Wonderful. He doesn't have any idea what he's up against."

Barely had she hung up when Jenny began dialing. She couldn't let herself hesitate or she might come up with a whole host of reasons not to take the risk, chief among them the fear that Logan had decided he could do without her and would not accept her effort at reconciliation.

Her hands were shaking as the phone rang at the school. She swallowed hard against the dryness of her throat and tried hard to think of exactly what she was going to say. But she might have spared herself the bother, for it wasn't Logan who answered.

"I thought you'd be calling about now," Maggie announced matter-of-factly. "How's everything there in Seattle?"

"Everything's fine." Resisting the impulse to ask how the housekeeper had known she would be in touch, she plowed on bravely. "Is Logan there?"

There was a moment's pause before Maggie said, "Why, no. He and the other men left five days ago."

"Left? For where?"

Silence again for endless seconds during which Jenny's heart began to hammer even more painfully. Finally, the housekeeper answered, "For Alaska. The start of the Mount McKinley expedition was moved up." Very gently, she added, "They should be starting the ascent right about now."

CHAPTER TWELVE

The afternoon flight to Anchorage was crowded. Businessmen in neat pinstripe suits shared space with oil rig workers in plaid shirts and workpants, tourists eagerly anticipating their visit to what many regarded as the country's last frontier, and a few big hard-eyed men who gave off the tacit understanding that their motives for making the trip should not be too closely examined.

There was an aura of excitement and anticipation not often encountered on routine commercial flights, a sense that they were all going somewhere the usual rules did not apply and where unlimited opportunities marched hand in hand with awesome challenges.

Many of the passengers were making immediate connections on the bush flights into the interior. By nightfall they would be in places Jenny could only dimly envision. Not for the first time since her hasty departure she wished she knew more about the city to which she was heading and the even more remote back country beyond.

Like most Washingtonians, she took it for granted that the rugged beauty of her state was unsurpassed anywhere else in the world. But coming in over Anchorage, she could not help but be struck by the stark majesty of its setting. The modern, bustling city framed on three sides by mountains was eloquent testament to the vision and tenacity of the men and women who had forged out a toehold on the edge of vastness almost beyond imagining.

The hotel where she was fortunate enough to get a room on such short notice looked out over Cook Inlet. When she explained her purpose in being there to the desk clerk, he proved unexpectedly helpful.

"Well, now," the tall young man began, "seems to be like the first thing you have to do is get yourself to Denali."

"Denali?"

"That's a town near the Mount McKinley National Park. This time of year the railroad goes there regularly, or you could rent a car."

"Could I fly in?"

"Yes, but that's a bit expensive. You'd have to charter a plane."

Jenny had already reconciled herself to the necessity of doing that. Time was far more precious to her than any amount of money.

"Can I arrange that through you?"

The young man nodded. "Certainly, but you realize that's only the first step. Then you'll have to get to the mountain itself. Park roads run to within about twenty-five miles of the base of the summit. I'm not sure how you'll get the rest of the way."

"I'll manage," Jenny said firmly. She had already come too far and there was too much at stake to turn back once she was so close to her objective. Hesitantly, she asked, "Do you know anything about a team of climbers attempting an ascent?"

"You mean the expedition that moved up its starting date because of the long-term weather forecasts?"

"That sounds like them."

"Well, if it is, my guess is they made the right decision. I've done a little climbing myself and I can tell you that

162

weather changes around here can be treacherous. McKinley is notorious for sudden bursts of blinding snow and high winds all year round." He shook his head admiringly. "Good luck to those guys. Even if the weather holds, they're going to need it."

Remembering that, Jenny spent a restless night tossing and turning in the unfamiliar bed. She had eaten dinner in her room so that she could concentrate on a book she found in the gift shop that described some of the earlier attempts to scale the mountain. What she read was the stuff of nightmares.

Notwithstanding the fact that several expeditions had made it to the top and returned without suffering casualties, most of the book was a litany of failed attempts, deadly falls, desperate rescue missions, and so on. What it boiled down to was that the mountain disdainfully tossed off its attempted vanquishers far more often than it yielded to them.

From the remarkable "sourdough" expedition of 1910, when a group of miners with no climbing experience but almost unbelievable luck managed to get all the way up the slope to the juncture of the north and south peaks, only to mistakenly scale the slightly smaller one, the mountain had attracted a myriad assortment of scientists, sportsmen, tricksters, and crazies.

The first expeditions had spent months simply reaching the base of the summit. That part of the ordeal, at least, had been considerably lessened. Now climbers customarily arrived by air, shuttled in as far as possible by daring bush pilots who did not let the frequently bad weather and often treacherous updrafts deter them.

But even with all the most advanced equipment and rigorous preparation, the mountain continued to claim lives. The seven members of Logan's party who had perished the year before were not even the most recent additions to the list. Two tragically ignorant young men had attempted an assault in early spring. They got as far as the Muldrow Glacier, the first great obstacle to any ascent, where their frozen bodies were found by rescuers.

After a largely sleepless night, Jenny was glad to make her way back to the airport to meet with the charter pilot the desk clerk recommended. Sam Barlow was a huge, gruff man who bore an uncanny resemblance to an irate grizzly bear. At first he met her request to be flown as close as possible to the climbers' main supply camp with outright rejection.

"You got no idea what you'd be getting into, lady. I can get you to the base of the mountain all right, even if we have to go in by helicopter. But from there to the main camp the only way is to climb. And I'm not talking about some little jaunt up the side of the hill. Logan sited the central supply drop at the top of Muldrow Glacier. That means real hard going over snow and ice. No way you'd make it."

Ignoring his discouragement, Jenny seized on a single part of what he had said. "Logan? You know him?"

Barlow unfolded his long legs from the desk on which they had remained propped despite her arrival and planted both his immense boot-shod feet on the floor with a resounding thud. For several moments he sucked thoughtfully at the plug of tobacco lodged in his bearded cheek before he finally nodded, "Yeah, me and Logan have hoisted a few beers together. But don't try to tell me he's expecting you up there 'cause I know damn well he isn't. Unless—"

He paused, studying her so intently that Jenny felt herself flush. The piercing black eyes deep-set beneath bushy brows seemed to see right through her. After a long moment a distressing scowl furrowed the pilot's brow.

"Logan kinda surprised me when I saw him this time.

He was too quiet, distracted. Didn't seem to be just that he was concentratin' on the climb. Seemed to be something else eatin' at him." His gaze sharpened. "You wouldn't have nothin' to do with that, would you?"

The question so flatly posed by a stranger was the same one that had haunted Jenny since learning that Logan was on the mountain. They had parted in anger, with him convinced that she did not truly love him. Once before he had joked of how thoughts of her distracted him under even the most demanding circumstances. Was that happening again, only from a far less pleasant cause and with potentially disastrous results?

"Yes," she said quietly, "I might have. I don't know for sure, but I think it would be best if I went to the base camp so that the support team could at least let Logan know I'm there. It might not matter to him at all, but on the other hand it may relieve his mind enough to let him concentrate completely on the climb."

Barlow leaned back in his big chair, which despite its size and apparent sturdiness creaked ominously under his weight. "So," he said a bit more gently, "you're willing to go all the way up there knowing he may not want you anymore?"

Hearing it put that bluntly, Jenny paled. She was well aware that it might be too late for her and Logan. She knew now that he truly had loved her, but her unwillingness to accept him as he was might have killed that love. If that were the case, she wouldn't be able to blame him despite all the grief and pain she would feel. No matter how much it hurt, she had to find out if he still cared. Not knowing was worse than anything else.

Unconsciously, her back straightened. She faced Barlow calmly. "Yes, I'm willing."

A tiny spark of admiration shone in the pilot's eyes. He got up and strode over to a computer printout tacked to the wall on which the latest weather information was displayed. Jenny waited, her hands clenched and her throat tight.

As absorbed as she was in the all-consuming necessity of reaching the base camp, some small portion of her mind still managed to register the more outrageous aspects of the situation. There she was a thoroughly modern, capable woman forced to depend on a burly denizen of the north who looked like a survivor from another age to escort her to what he undoubtedly thought of as "her man."

But what, she had to ask herself, was so ridiculous about that? Logan was her man, in the most elemental way possible. Whether he was willing to acknowledge it or not, she knew they belonged together so completely that there was no room left over for consideration of the particular standards of any single time or place.

Perhaps because Barlow lived in such close contact with the eternal power of nature, he was able to recognize the forces at work within her almost as clearly as she did herself. Or at least she had to hope he did, and that they would be strong enough to sway him.

By the time he finally turned back to her, Jenny was almost trembling. She could hardly bring herself to meet his eyes, so concerned was she about what she would see there.

Relief surged through her when he said, "Looks clear enough. But there's no point us takin' off till you've got somethin' better to wear." His eyes ran over her tailored wool slacks, silk blouse, and cashmere pullover derisively. "Or were you figurin' to climb up the mountain gussied up like that?"

Jenny was too grateful to let his mockery offend her. "No," she said quietly, "I wasn't. I'll have to go to a sporting goods store and get some different clothes."

"You know what you'll need?"

166

"I . . . think so. . . ."

"You'll have to do better than that. Once you get up on the slope, there won't be any of them little boutiques to run into for somethin' you forgot." A mournful sigh escaped him as he considered the mess she would undoubtedly make of outfitting herself. With the air of a man about to make the ultimate sacrifice, he said, "Guess I'd best take you shopping."

Jenny prided herself on being able to get in and out of a store quickly. Her busy life left no time for browsing and demanded that she select everything necessary for her wardrobe and apartment in the least time possible. Even so, she was unprepared for the lightning assault Sam Barlow led her on as they tore their way through several stores specializing in mountaineering gear.

It was fortunate that he was apparently well known to the owners and staff, otherwise his brusk, impatient orders and surly instructions might have gotten more than a few backs up.

Within a matter of hours she was fully outfitted with everything from thermal underwear to flannel shirts, oiled wool sweaters, insulated, waterproof pants, a down-filled parka, thick socks, and climbing boots. She was lectured on the dangers of frostbite, given a quick course on the topography of Mount McKinley, and even provided with an emergency ration kit in case, as Barlow wickedly suggested, "Logan decides you ain't worth feeding."

With the exception of a few similar comments, the pilot proved himself to be surprisingly gracious. The gleam in his eye was enough to tell Jenny that he found her attractive. But for the fact that she was clearly another man's woman, she might have had trouble fending him off. As it was, Barlow would deliver her to his friend safe and sound, though he left no doubt that whatever happened to her after that was strictly up to Logan.

The pilot waited downstairs in the hotel lobby while Jenny threw the few things she had used the night before back into her bag and checked out. She was well aware that once Logan learned of her presence, he might order her sent straight back to Anchorage, in which case she would be wiser to hold on to the room. But she refused to leave herself any escape route. Instead, she stored her belongings in Sam Barlow's office as he checked out the plane and filed his flight plan.

Moments later they were roaring down the runway in a slightly battered four-seater whose powerful engines more than made up for the lack of amenities. The plane needed only a few hundred feet to reach take-off speed. Jenny barely had a chance to breathe before they were surging into the crystal-clear sky.

Anchorage fell away behind them, quickly eclipsed by the mountains and the vast panorama of rugged landscape behind them. The noise in the cockpit made it impossible to talk, which seemed to suit Barlow fine, although he did unbend enough to offer Jenny coffee from an oversize thermos and a sandwich so thick she had trouble getting it into her mouth.

Despite her anxiousness, the food was welcome. She knew the flight was only the first stage of an arduous journey that would tax her resources to their limit.

By afternoon they had set down at the landing strip inside Mount McKinley National Park and transferred to a helicopter, which, as Barlow had promised, he managed to bring to within just a few miles of the base camp.

Throughout the last stage of their air journey, Jenny's eyes were riveted on the colossus dominating sky and earth. Although much of the mountain was hidden from view by the clouds that almost always obscured both peaks, what she could see of it made all ordinary perceptions of scale useless. She could well understand why the

168

native Indian tribes had called it the "Home of the Sun," and why the Russians had more succinctly dubbed it the "Great One." A slight smile curved her mouth as she considered that only Americans would have the effrontery to name such a marvel of nature for a president of doubtful achievement.

Barlow had brought another pilot along, who would return the helicopter to the landing strip and wait for instructions about picking them up again. Before the two men parted, they double-checked both their radios to be sure they would have no difficulty getting in contact.

As Jenny watched the chopper dart back into the sky, a sense of mingled excitement and dread filled her. Their last link with civilization was, if not broken, certainly stretched thin. They were on their own, surrounded by rugged wilderness, with only their own strength and skill to get them to the nearest human habitation, the base camp on Muldrow Glacier.

At first the going was not that rough. The ground was covered with loose gravel and strewn with boulders. Meltwater made every surface glisten, but did not impede their progress. They made excellent time, but Jenny did not let herself get overconfident. Up ahead, stretching out before them, was the vast expanse of the glacier. They would only have to cross a small part of it to reach the camp, but even that would be a difficult undertaking for her.

"All right, now," Barlow said as he paused briefly. The ground beneath their boots had begun to crunch about an hour back as they entered the region of eternal snow and ice. Jenny's clothes kept her comfortably warm, but she was grateful that her backpack was fairly light. She listened attentively as Barlow said, "From here on it gets steadily tougher. You say Logan taught you to climb, so I'm willing to bet you've got enough sense to do as you're told. We stay roped together at all times and you don't take a step off the path I set. Got it?"

"Got it," Jenny confirmed. She had no intention of trying to test her climbing skills even against this lowest part of the range. It was enough that Barlow was apparently almost as skilled a mountaineer as Logan himself and that he had followed the same route many times before. She was willing to trust him completely, though she did cast a worried look at the sun, which had moved far to the west.

Barlow caught her look and grinned. "Don't worry, little lady. I've got no intention of getting stuck out here tonight. We'll be at camp well before sunset."

Relieved, Jenny nodded. They moved on in silence, both concentrating strictly on the demands of the climb.

True to his word, there were still several hours of daylight left when they rounded another bend and sighted the cluster of snow-encrusted tents that formed the base camp. About a dozen people were moving about, some working on equipment stacked in neat piles, others arriving or departing on skis with heavy packs they were transporting to the next depot higher up the slopes. Everything looked extremely well organized, which was hardly surprising considering the experience of the climbers and the rigorous standards of their leader.

Jenny shivered slightly, not from the cold that was beginning to bite through her garments or even from the fatigue creeping over her, but from sheer gut fear about how Logan would react when he found she was there. Deke or whoever else was in charge of the base camp would certainly radio the news to him. No matter how many thousands of feet higher up the mountain he might be, she had no doubt she would be able to feel his reaction as clearly as if he were standing next to her.

For the first time since deciding she could not remain

in Seattle while he was risking his life on the mountain, Jenny doubted the wisdom of what she was doing. Not that there was any chance of withdrawing. They had already been spotted and the parka-clad figures were turning to look at them.

Sensing her apprehension, Barlow spoke more gently than she had yet heard him. "Come on, then. No point standin' around here when the food and shelter's down there."

As they came down the slope, one of the figures in the camp detached himself from the rest and moved forward to meet them. Barlow was far enough out in front that the two had several moments to talk before Jenny reached them. She was almost at their side when the pilot turned, flashed her a sardonic grin, and marched off toward the tents.

Left alone, she took a deep breath while making a last-ditch effort to find the right words that would explain her presence. She might have saved herself the effort.

The man Barlow had been talking with impatiently pushed back the hood of his parka. Silver curls glinted in the sun above a ruggedly tan face set in hard, grim lines.

His voice a low growl, Logan demanded, "Just what the hell do you think you're doing here?"

CHAPTER THIRTEEN

Jenny didn't even try to answer him right away. She was too busy staring at him, drinking in every detail of his appearance. He looked tired and angry, but otherwise perfectly all right. Slowly, as she realized he was truly safe, a smile wreathed her face.

"Logan . . . you're here . . ." She glanced toward the mountain looming over them. "You aren't . . . up there . . ."

Her voice trailed off. The icy look in his eyes that was at least a match for their frozen surroundings did not encourage her to continue. She couldn't bring herself to ask why he was still at the base camp for fear of hearing that the ascent had simply been delayed and that he would be leaving soon. Waiting for him would be bad enough, but to actually have to watch him begin the ascent that might end in his death . . .

"We're not talking about me," Logan snarled. "I asked you what you're doing here."

A dull flush stained Jenny's cheeks, which were pale with cold and weariness. She certainly hadn't expected a royal welcome, but neither was she willing to sit still for such blatant rudeness.

Cruelly provoked at a time when her defenses were very low, she couldn't bear to make herself even more vulnerable by revealing the true purpose of her visit. Instead, she said, "I decided this would be a good finish for my story, so I came to cover the climb."

The moment the words were out, she bit her lip, praying Logan wouldn't believe them. But he did. His face tightened even further and the big hands at his sides clenched.

"Then you can just turn around and take yourself back where you came from, honey, because there's no way I'm going to let you or anyone else distract the team or try to exploit what we're doing here."

"*Exploit!* Since when is news coverage exploitation?"

His eyes hardened to the consistency of granite as they moved over her callously. "Since it came wrapped up in complete disregard for anything beyond your career."

For once in her life, words failed Jenny. She stared at him in shock. How could he so wantonly distort what had happened between them? Not for a minute did she believe he really thought she was capable of the kind of relationship they had shared without caring for him deeply. But the mere fact that he was willing to suggest as much hurt badly.

"*Why you b-b . . .*"

"Careful, Jenny. You can't afford a temper tantrum right now. Save your energy for getting your cute little butt out of my camp."

The possibility that he might actually be serious about her leaving tempered her anger. Dazedly, she shook her head. "You know there's no way to reach the landing site before nightfall. No matter how you feel about me, I can't believe you'd subject Sam Barlow to a night on the mountainside."

Logan frowned. He had spoken impulsively, knowing full well he wouldn't allow anyone to attempt a descent so late in the day, especially not a relatively inexperienced climber like Jenny. Reluctantly, he took in the unmistakable signs of cold and fatigue that she was trying to hide behind a stubborn mask of pride. Unwilling admiration darted through him as he realized that though she was clearly ready to drop, she wasn't about to ask him for help.

Refusing to give in to the concern he felt for her, Logan grumbled, "Oh, all right. You can stay until morning. But keep out of the way."

Without another look at her, he left her standing where she was and went back to work.

Numbed by the combined effects of his anger and her exhaustion, Jenny moved forward slowly. She had no idea where she should go or what she should do. Her normally clear, decisive mind was simply overwhelmed. Not even the gnawing demand of her body for food, warmth, and rest could penetrate the fog of her unhappiness. She was profoundly grateful that Logan was safe, but she was also painfully aware of how angry he was and how her own defensive lie had further fueled his wrath.

Why hadn't she told him the truth, or at least kept silent? Why had she lashed out in a way guaranteed to make everything worse between them?

Baffled by her own behavior, Jenny stopped several yards from the portable kerosene heater that provided some measure of comfort in the frozen wasteland. But not to her, for she hadn't even noticed that she was well outside the circle of its warmth.

It was left to Sam Barlow to draw her closer, pull her backpack off, and push a hot mug of soup into her gloved hand. "Here, drink this. Don't you remember what I told you about getting dehydrated at this altitude?"

Jenny barely heard him. She sipped the soup automatically, not noticing that it burned her tongue. She was so tired. . . .

"You need some rest," Sam growled. "Better find a place to lie down."

She glanced around, realizing that he was right. She

wouldn't be able to stay on her feet much longer. Work was winding down in the camp. The men who formed the support team were getting ready for supper before retiring to their tents for the night. Neither she nor Sam had brought such accommodation for themselves. Knowing they would reach the bivouac before dark, there hadn't been any reason to do so. But now . . .

"Where are you sleeping?" she asked tentatively.

"I'm bunking in with one of the guys." A wry gleam shone in his eyes as he added, "Guess you'd better do the same."

"Is-isn't there a spare tent?"

"Nope. Just about everyone's in a double right now."

"But there are a few singles left?"

"Only one."

She had a sinking feeling what he was going to say even before she asked, "Whose is that?"

Sam grinned. "Logan's, of course. The way your luck's running, how could it be anyone else's?"

Jenny groaned softly. She had a horrible image of herself having to plead with a recalcitrant Logan to let her share his shelter.

Seeing her dismay, the ever-helpful Sam couldn't resist a suggestion, "Tell you what, I'll bunk with Logan and you can bed down with one of the other guys. How's that sound?"

Appalling, but she just might not have any other choice. She was about to say as much when a deep voice behind her interrupted.

"It sounds lousy," Logan declared. Without looking at her, he added flatly, "Jenny stays with me."

Sam shrugged good-naturedly. He seemed well-satisfied with the success of his ploy. "Well, if that's the way you want it . . ."

"It isn't. But that doesn't make any difference." Finally

condescending to glance at her, Logan smiled humorously. "Besides, I wouldn't want to inflict her on anyone else."

Sam laughed heartily, but Jenny was not amused. She knew she was being deliberately provoked, but she couldn't stop her instinctive response. Bitingly, she said, "I couldn't allow you to make such a sacrifice."

Logan shrugged disdainfully. "You don't have any alternative."

"Yes, I do. I'll . . . I'll sleep outside."

They both knew that was patently ridiculous, but Jenny refused to back down. The smug male look in his eyes enraged her. He thought he could treat her with unrestrained contempt and still force her to be grateful for the tiny scrap of comfort he deigned to throw at her.

She had swallowed all the pride and hurt she would. From now on he would have to meet her halfway.

Logan seemed to sense he had pushed her as far as he could, for after a moment he said, "You try it and I'll tan your backside so that you won't be able to sleep comfortably for a month, here or anywhere else."

Determined that they were going to be absolutely clear on why she was sleeping in his tent, Jenny demanded, "Are you seriously saying you'll force me to bunk with you?"

Tempted though he was to mutter something about how it had never required force to bring them together, Logan thought better of it. The dangerous glint in Jenny's indigo eyes warned of exactly how she would respond to such a sally. Damn, but she was a remarkable woman! By rights she should be dropping from exhaustion and glad of any help he offered. Instead, she glared at him defiantly and made it clear she wasn't taking a step until he showed some modicum of courtesy.

"No," he admitted at length, "that's not what I'm saying. After dark the temperature here falls well below zero. We've been lucky the last couple of days not to get fresh snow, but the wind gusts make up for that. You wouldn't last half an hour outside, and we both know it. So since we are both reasonable adults"—his skeptical glance made it clear he really wasn't sure about that—"you will share my tent. Agreed?"

Reluctantly, Jenny nodded. She had held out as long as she possibly could. Lifting her backpack, she followed him to the snug shelter set on the leeward side of an immense snowdrift. Just the effort of getting there was almost more than she could manage. Her pack, which had felt so light that morning, now seemed weighted down by boulders. Her head throbbed and every muscle in her body cried out for rest. Only by doggedly putting one foot in front of the other was she able to keep up with him.

Slipping inside the tent, she glanced around nervously. It was so small that it was impossible to stand upright. A sleeping bag took up almost half the available space. A tiny stove gave off a glow of heat that made her skin tingle. Logan's own pack rested against the far end.

Still standing outside, he said, "Make yourself comfortable. You don't look in any shape to join the rest of us at dinner, so I'll bring you something."

Jenny wanted to object that she didn't need any special treatment, but the words were beyond her. Barely had she unrolled her own sleeping bag and pulled off her parka when she was fast asleep.

Logan came back half an hour later. He had eaten quickly and skipped his usual custom of joining in the after-dinner conversation with the other men. Though he didn't like to admit it, he was worried about Jenny. He wanted to make sure she was all right.

Entering the tent, he stared down at the slender figure stretched out on top of the sleeping bag. A scowl darkened his forehead. She hadn't even had the sense to get inside it! Putting down the insulated container of food he had brought, he shook her roughly.

"Get up, Jenny. You have to eat, and you can't sleep like that anyway."

She protested groggily, but did as he said. He held her light weight propped up against him as she managed to eat a good portion of the hearty beef stew and drink a cup of cocoa. But before he could convince her to have another, the cup almost slipped from her fingers as she drifted back into sleep.

Shaking his head ruefully, he eased her back onto the sleeping bag. Against his better judgment, the harsh lines of his face relaxed as he looked at her. Her rich dark hair was spread out in glistening waves, stark against the dull khaki of the tent floor. Her face was pale, the thick fringe of her lashes casting shadows on her high-boned cheeks. His throat tightened as he considered how fragile she looked.

Gritting his teeth, he removed her boots, then went to work on the rest of her clothes. If she slept in the heavy sweater, shirt, and pants, the air inside the sleeping bag would never be warmed by her body heat, and she would therefore feel chilled all night. Novice climbers always resisted the idea that it was better to remove clothes in such cold weather, but the tactic worked.

Jenny was left with nothing but her long underwear, which fit snugly along every inch of her slender but curvaceous figure. The buttons at the top were undone, affording him a glimpse of the ripe curve of her breasts. In the cool air of the tent her nipples hardened reflexively, reminding Logan all too clearly of how they felt beneath his hand and mouth.

A low groan broke from him as he slipped her inside the sleeping bag and resolutely zipped it up. Once she was out of sight, he felt a little better, at least enough to neatly fold up her clothes. Knowing they would be uncomfortable to put on the next morning if left out all night, he reached for her pack to put them away.

Jenny was deeply asleep when she felt someone embracing her. A soft moan rippled from her as she rose from the snug comfort of her sleeping bag. But it turned to a sigh of pleasure as she was quickly wrapped in hard, warm arms, drawn tight against a big, powerful body, and gently stroked until she drifted easily back into her dreams.

She woke hours later, as the first faint rim of light was showing above the eastern horizon, to find herself curled so closely next to Logan that not a breath of air could move between them. Her head lay on his chest, the rhythmic beat of his heart sounding just beneath her ear.

How had she gotten there? Surely she hadn't been so weak as to go to him in the night? How he would mock her if he realized what the desperate yearnings of her heart and body had driven her to.

Stirring gingerly, she tried to untangle herself without waking him. If she could only get back to her own sleeping bag, or better yet escape the tent altogether . . .

"Good morning."

The low, faintly husky voice reverberated through Jenny with the force of a gunshot. She looked up hurriedly, straight into Logan's quicksilver eyes.

"Uh . . . good morning . . ."

"How did you sleep?" he inquired pleasantly.

"F-fine, I guess."

Beneath a night's growth of golden stubble, his sensual mouth twitched. "I should hope so. You seemed quite— comfortable."

Flushing, Jenny lowered he gaze. Which didn't do all that much good, since she ended up staring at his powerful

179

chest clearly outlined by the thin covering of thermal cotton he wore. "Did I . . . that is, how did I get over here?"

"Don't you remember?" he taunted, but with an odd note of gentleness that surprised her.

"If I did," she muttered, "I wouldn't ask."

Logan's smile faded. His expression became serious as he said, "I put you in with me. Partly because you were so worn out that you seemed to be having trouble staying warm on your own and partly because I just wanted to hold you."

"W-why would you want to do that?"

He chuckled softly. "Because you feel good."

Jenny's flush deepened. She couldn't understand why he was teasing her like this when just a few hours before he had been so callous. "I—I thought you were angry at me."

Logan didn't answer directly. Instead, he said very softly, "Jenny, last night I put your clothes away so they'd be warm enough to put on this morning. I couldn't help but notice you didn't bring your camera with you, or any notebooks. Heck, I couldn't even find a pencil." His arms tightened around her, his voice becoming low and caressing. "Would you mind telling me how you plan to cover this story without all your usual paraphernalia?"

A long sigh escaped her. He had found her out and she couldn't pretend to be anything but glad. Meeting his gaze bravely, she said, "I don't, Logan. When I said that was my reason for being here, I was lying. The truth is I came up here to tell you I'm sorry for being so insensitive and to ask if you can forgive me."

"Does that mean," Logan said slowly, "that you no longer mind about my climbing?"

"No," Jenny admitted. "I'm still terribly afraid of your being in danger, but I realize now that just because I love

180

you, I don't have any right to try to control your life. I was asking you to give up something too essential to you. You were right to refuse."

"Regardless of the cost to you?"

"I'm not claiming the price isn't high, Logan. It is. But losing you is far worse. I want to be with you even if that means having to live with my own fears."

He was silent for so long that she became anxious and looked up to try to guess what he might be thinking. The answer was written clearly in his glittering silver eyes and in the tender curve of his mouth.

"Jenny . . ." he breathed softly. "Sweet Jenny. You're more than I deserve."

At his words the first sparks of profound relief and joy began to surge through her. Shakily, she said, "I'm not. You're the one who's special."

She got no further. Logan's hard yet infinitely gentle lips silenced her. Against her mouth he whispered, "I love you. These days without you have been hell. I wanted to follow you to Seattle, but the climb got moved up. I was planning to call as soon as I got off this blasted mountain, to find out if you still wanted anything to do with me. When I saw you standing there with Sam, I thought I was dreaming." He chuckled softly. "The cold and ice do that to a man sometimes. Hallucinations aren't all that uncommon, sort of like mirages in the desert. I thought that was what you were, a beautiful hallucination come to torment me."

"And instead I promptly announced I was only here for a story."

He shook her lightly. "I could have cheerfully strangled you for that, except that I kept thinking of how much I wanted to do this"—his lips touched hers tenderly—"and this . . ." A big, gentle hand cupped her breast, the thumb rubbing sensuously over her taut nipple. ". . . and this

181

. . ." His powerful body moved against her, making her intimately aware of exactly what he had in mind.

Any effort at feminine coyness vanished as her own body responded in kind. Without a second thought she murmured, "Can we? The others? Is the climb going to start soon?"

Logan drew back slightly, enough so that he could look down at her without breaking the contact all along the length of their bodies. He smiled wryly. "I really do have trouble explaining myself where you're concerned, don't I?"

"What do you mean?"

His hand nuzzled her cheek tenderly, lean, bronze fingers trailing a line of fire down her throat to the sensitive hollow that he kissed lingeringly. Her heart was beating at double-time before he said, "The climb has already started. With luck Deke and the rest will make the summit by this afternoon. I'm just leading the support team."

Jenny's eyes widened with shock. "But it was so important to you!"

"You're more important, much more. You're the most important thing in the world. Nothing else even comes close. I finally admitted that to myself after you left, when I had time to realize what an idiot I'd been."

Gazing down into the indigo pools misted by joyful tears, he said softly, "A lifetime with you won't be long enough. I can't bear to waste a single precious hour, let alone take the risk of throwing away everything we could have together just to conquer another mountain."

The full impact of what was happening between them turned Jenny radiant. Loving elation shimmered through her. Her eyes glowed like sapphire fires as she smiled alluringly. "Is there something else you'd rather conquer?"

Logan's lusty laugh left no doubt that there was indeed,

182

and that his victory would be hers as well. Heedless of the tight confines of the sleeping bag, of the hard ground beneath them, or anything other than their ardent love, he drew her to him.

CHAPTER FOURTEEN

"Here's to the guy who stayed at the bottom but still managed to get to the top," Deke proclaimed, lifting his glass of champagne in salute.

His sally was met with cheers by the rest of the climbing team, all of whom were gathered back at Logan's school to celebrate both his marriage and their successful ascent of Mount McKinley.

"I don't know," Sam Barlow grumbled good-naturedly, shaking his head. "Seems to me you fellows did all the work and he had all the fun."

"Too true," Deke laughed. His gaze fell on Jenny, looking glorious in a dress of shimmering blue silk that perfectly matched both her eyes and the sapphire of her engagement ring, now joined by a wide gold wedding band. "And to think," he sighed mournfully, "I actually felt sorry for our intrepid leader when he said he wasn't going to make the climb."

Lifting his wife's hand, Logan pressed a gentle kiss to her palm before he said, "When you get a few more miles on you, Deke, you'll find out there are some challenges in life more worth pursuing than any mountain." He grinned boldly. "And certainly more difficult!"

"Who's difficult?" Jenny demanded flippantly. "Not me."

"Oh, no," her husband drawled. "You're always even-tempered, reasonable, calm, submissive . . ."

"*Submissive!*" Jenny repeated in mock outrage. "Now listen here, if you think I'm going to stand still for that . . ."

"She's a challenge all right," Deke said cordially.

"A real spitfire," Sam agreed.

"You've got your hands full now," another climber chimed in.

"Better start as you plan to go on," a fourth advised.

"You think so?" Logan asked, glancing around at the men. They all nodded somberly, despite their teasing smiles.

He shrugged philosophically. "Guess you're right." Before Jenny could open her mouth to insist the joke had gone far enough, he took the champagne glass from her, set it on the table, and in a single agile movement, tossed her over his broad shoulder.

Her indignant shriek was drowned out by the encouraging shouts of the men, several of whom thoughtfully stepped forward to open the door. Even the minister who had performed the ceremony just a short time before smiled benignly. He could well afford to, since what he was quite certain was about to occur was now thoroughly blessed by both man and God.

"Save us some cake," Logan called as he strode down the path to the waiting jeep, calmly ignoring the irate bundle of femininity locked snugly against him.

"I'll get you for this," Jenny muttered the moment he set her down in the seat, but she was smiling as she said it. Logan's desire for them to be alone was perfectly matched by her own. Despite the passion-filled days and nights they had shared in the week since rediscovering each other, it was difficult to be unable to touch for even a few hours.

The ceremony, simple though it was, had seemed endless. Jenny could hardly bear to think what it would have been like if both Logan's family and her own hadn't been so understanding about their desire to be married swiftly. Of course, they had promised to visit both Philadelphia and Boston, and they would, but not for a while yet.

Staring down at the bouquet of lilies sent by Kirsten, Jenny smiled. Their trip would have to include a stopover in New York, made all the more urgent by the fact that her friend was about to take the matrimonial plunge herself.

When Jenny had called to tell her she and Logan were back together, Kirsten evinced no surprise. She only said, "I knew you were too smart to walk away from something that special. I'm just surprised I've got enough guts to go through with it myself."

But she was, at Charlie's heartfelt urgings and to the relief of his horde of relatives all of whom seemed to have come round to admitting she was definitely good enough for him.

"Do you think we're part of a trend?" Jenny mused as she considered the odds against both of them getting married in such a short span of time.

"Definitely. In fact, as soon as you come down to earth enough to work, I want you to write an article about the revival of romance. Think you can handle it?"

"I don't know. . . . It'll take a lot of research."

Kirsten laughed tolerantly. "I have faith you'll manage." Just before she hung up, she added, "Of course, Logan may die of exhaustion, but at least it'll be for a good cause."

"What's so funny?" he asked as Jenny chuckled softly.

"Oh, nothing. . . . I was just thinking about work."

"*Work!* Here I've just swept you off your feet and am

186

carrying you away to have my wicked will with you, and you're thinking about work?"

Laughing, she told him about her new assignment, concluding, "So you see, I'm really depending on you to help me on it."

"My pleasure, ma'am. It's a tough job, but a man's got to do what a man's got to do."

"Hmmm." Nestling against him, Jenny teased the silvery curls near his ear. "Are you sure you're up to it? I mean, it will require sustained effort."

Logan flashed her a look that made it quite clear where such comments would get her. Moments later he pulled into the driveway of their house. Coming around the other side of the jeep, he scooped her up and carried her inside.

"Now, isn't it fortunate," he purred into her ear, "that we decided not to go on to the fishing cabin until tomorrow?"

"Oh, I don't know," Jenny hedged, greatly enjoying the sensation of being held against his chest. "It's a nice night for a drive."

"It's a better night for something else," he informed her bluntly as he walked straight through the living room and up the stairs to the sleeping loft.

Setting Jenny on her feet, Logan took a step back, just enough to give him a clear view of her. His big hands pushed aside the jacket of the elegantly tailored suit he wore, to rest on his narrow hips. Quicksilver eyes gleamed as he ordered, "Get undressed."

A shiver ran along Jenny's spine. If anyone had ever told her she would enjoy playing such games . . . But with Logan, she was quickly discovering there was no room for inhibition.

Privately telling herself she had missed her calling as an actress, she slowly, reluctantly, kicked off her shoes and reached under her skirt to pull off her panty hose. His eyes never moved from her as she unzipped the dress and slid it from her shoulders. When it lay in a pool of blue silk at her feet, she stood before him clad only in her lacy bra and minuscule panties.

A pulse throbbed in his jaw as he surveyed her glowing beauty. His voice was almost harsh as he demanded, "Take off everything."

Her fingers shook as she complied. The air felt cool against her nakedness. His unrelenting gaze made her fight the urge to cover herself.

Touching her only with his eyes, Logan murmured thickly, "You're exquisite. Every inch of you. Each time I see you I realize that all over again." As he spoke he was hastily removing his own clothes. Within seconds he was as naked as she except for the briefs covering his straining manhood.

Jenny swallowed tightly. When he told her to get on the bed, she obeyed unhesitantly.

"Like I said," Logan teased her as he removed his last garment and lowered himself beside her, "submissive."

"You think so?" Jenny murmured.

Logan smiled. "You could always prove me wrong."

That was a challenge no woman worth the name would refuse. Her small hands settled on his shoulders, caressing the powerful muscles there before gently pushing him down on the mattress.

When he was stretched out before her, Jenny sat back on her heels. Her indigo eyes surveyed him every bit as thoroughly as he had her before she at last allowed her hands and mouth to touch him.

Dropping feather-light kisses over his face and throat, she worked her way down to tease the male nipples that hardened instantly at her caress. An irresistible tremor ran through him as her hands followed the path of golden hair over his broad chest to his flat abdomen and beyond.

When her mouth followed, he could no longer contain himself. He reached out, only to have her laughingly evade his hands. "I'm not done yet. I think you need more convincing before you decide you don't really want a submissive wife."

Logan could only groan in response as she stroked the long line of his legs clear to his feet. When her mouth traced the same route, at last reaching the sensitive skin of his inner thighs, his big hands tangled in her hair. With consummate skill and tenderness, she expressed her love in the most enticing ways possible.

He stood it through long, erotic moments until he could bear no more. A deep, utterly male growl rumbled from him as he seized Jenny's slender hips and flipped her onto her back.

Hovering over her, he grinned dangerously. "Do you know what happens when you tease a man that far?"

"Yes," Jenny purred, savoring the weight of him as he held her trapped beneath him. She breathed in sharply as his knee thrust between her legs, urging them open.

"Good," Logan growled. "Then this won't surprise you."

As his mouth took hers with heated urgency, his tongue plunged deep. Warm, skillful hands moved up her slender hips and waist to cup the fullness of her breasts. Gently kneading the taut nipples, he teased her through long, enthralling moments before at last letting her feel the tender lapping of his tongue and the exquisite pressure of his mouth on the aching peaks.

Slipping his hair-rough thighs between hers, he made her acutely aware of his extreme arousal. Jenny cried softly, urging the culmination of their love. Again covering her mouth with his own, Logan heeded her plea.

He entered her in a single thrust, driving deeply into her

womanhood. A shocked gasp tore from her even as she yielded to the delicious sensations he provoked.

Once having claimed what was his alone, he moved more slowly, drawing out her pleasure to the utmost. Jenny was almost crazed with need when they at last broke through the furthest limits of ecstasy to shattering release.

Temporarily sated, they slept briefly, only to wake and love again and again throughout the night. Logan was alternately tender and rough, giving and demanding. His caresses brought her shattering joy even as they left no room for the slightest remnant of modesty or restraint. Reveling in the pleasure he gave her, she was unbridled in her desire to return the same depth of rapture to him.

When they at last fell into a deep sleep, it lasted until well after dawn. They did not wake again until the sun had chased away the stars and was climbing high over Devil's Summit, nature's witness to the love that soared higher than the greatest mountain and would last far longer.

Candlelight
Ecstasy Romances™

$1.95 each